"Damn it, Red, you're killing me."

With her tongue Sienna trailed a path down A.J.'s rigid stomach to the snap of his pants. "If I take them off, I'll take them off my way."

A.J. moaned softly, caressing her hair, her shoulders.

She gripped his waistband and tugged; the navy whites fell to the floor. She kissed the satin-smooth skin at the edge of his briefs. "I don't think these are standard navy issue...."

His breathing was ragged, but Sienna couldn't stop. With a quick move, she pulled the underwear down.

A.J. groaned.

Cupping his hard, hot arousal in her hands, she said softly, "No, sirree, this is *not* standard in any way."

Blaze™

Dear Reader,

Hers to Take is the first book in my miniseries Women Who Dare—where three friends dare each other to taste the forbidden and get a souvenir!

A. J. Camacho wants to find his brother and Sienna Parker wants to get dangerous guns off the streets of San Diego. Trouble is A.J.'s brother seems like the guy who took the guns and Sienna, being a rules and regs cop, is going after him.

Mixing a free-thinking U.S. Navy SEAL with a straight-arrow cop naturally leads them to conflict. Except my characters can't help an intense attraction, hot passion and heightened emotions from bringing them closer together.

I hope you enjoy reading about my tough and tender characters and how they overcome their own personal fears. I love to hear from my readers so please drop me an e-mail at www.karenanders.com.

Enjoy!

Karen Anders

P.S. In November, look for #111 *Yours to Seduce,* book 2 in the Women Who Dare miniseries.

Books by Karen Anders

HARLEQUIN BLAZE
22—THE BARE FACTS
43—HOT ON HER TAIL
74—THE DIVA DIARIES

HERS TO TAKE

Karen Anders

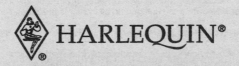

HARLEQUIN®

TORONTO • NEW YORK • LONDON
AMSTERDAM • PARIS • SYDNEY • HAMBURG
STOCKHOLM • ATHENS • TOKYO • MILAN • MADRID
PRAGUE • WARSAW • BUDAPEST • AUCKLAND

To my best American hero
Thanks, Dad

A special acknowledgment
to Captain Bill Pattee, USN (retired),
for his assistance with all things Navy.
I would also like to thank Brenda and Tom Fish
for help with the San Diego area.
Any mistakes are mine.

ISBN 0-373-79107-0

HERS TO TAKE

1

NORMALLY, SIENNA PARKER wouldn't mind a gorgeous, 210-pound muscular male straddling her hips.

Except this guy wasn't a lover and he had her pinned flat on her back. His arm was across her throat and Sienna could barely breathe. When she looked up into his face, he looked back with a pair of narrowed electric blue eyes, fringed by long, dark lashes. Thick black, temple-cut hair hung around his forehead, grazing his ears. For a moment, just a tiny moment, she lost herself in the look of him.

She blinked, realizing that the only opportunity she had was to go for the groin. Normally, that wouldn't bother her, either, but in this case, she expected to do some damage. Her knee came up, but the guy was quick. As quick as he'd been when she'd approached David Buckner's apartment, found the door ajar, and suspicious rustlings going on inside. It had made her worried enough to pick up her radio and call for backup.

"Who are you and what are you doing here?" His voice rasped out.

"Detective Sienna Parker, San Diego Police Department,'' she whispered around the pressure on her throat.

She should have waited for her backup, instead of worrying about losing a lead. She couldn't follow any leads if she was dead, all the more reason to never go against the rule book again.

He immediately eased up on her neck. Surprise, then wariness, showed on his handsome face. ''You're a cop?''

Now and forever! Detective Sienna Parker always played by the rule book. Her friends said that if she could, she'd have No Buts tattooed on her behind.

Keenly aware of the choke hold on her neck and the heat radiating from his body, she regained some of her equilibrium. After all, she was a decorated cop, young, smart and even though he had the drop on her right now, things could change fast. She threatened, ''You got it and just so you know, you're facing arrest charges for assaulting an officer.''

And he'd been very good at assault.

Even though she'd been off duty, she'd followed procedure, reached back and pulled out her 9mm Smith & Wesson and thumbed off the safety. Gently, she'd pushed the door open and slipped inside, the gun pointed straight out in front of her. She'd walked into the living room and discovered a man at Buckner's desk, looking through the contents. As stealthily as possible, she'd approached the man from behind.

But before she could say, "Freeze, police!" he moved faster than any man she'd ever seen before.

Her gun was gone. Kicked out of her hands, numbing her fingers and her wrist in an exceptional kick that he performed with ease and grace. Then he was on her, bearing her to the rug, his forearm across her throat. She looked up at him, realizing he could snap her neck like a twig.

"Let me see your badge."

Sienna reached down between their bodies, the back of her hand sliding along hard packed muscle until she reached her blazer pocket. She pulled the leather jacket free, brought it up to his face and flipped it open.

He studied the oblong shield and then looked into her eyes. "I didn't know you were a cop. I don't like people sneaking up behind me with guns. Makes me testy." His shoulders blocked out the desk and the window beyond. All she could see was part of the curtains. But she could hear a siren getting closer. Her backup was on the way and if they found her like this, she'd never live it down. Her fellow officers loved to rib her, first because she was a woman and second because she'd sped through the patrol ranks and made detective faster than any man in her graduating class at the academy.

"You know what makes me testy, mister? Being restrained by some guy who's just committed a B and E. Who the hell are you?"

She felt his powerful stomach muscles clench in an effort to rise. "Lieutenant A. J. Camacho, United States Navy."

"Well, Lieutenant A. J. Camacho of the United States Navy...get off me!" She wasn't shouting, but there was a core of steel accompanying every word.

A.J. got off her and reached out his hand to help her up. Sienna felt it the moment she placed her hand in his—electricity, heat, chemistry. Whatever one wanted to call it. It was there in the air crackling between them.

With a swift pull, he had her on her feet. He stood with ease; his unzipped leather bomber jacket revealing a blue chambray shirt open at the collar, exposing a strong neck. She could see a glint of his dog tags along with some kind of gold medallion around his throat that she immediately recognized as a Saint Christopher medal. Standing, he was impressively built and had muscles that were exquisitely honed. Snug jeans molded down long muscular legs and ended at scuffed black boots.

He walked over to retrieve her gun. Sienna moved fast, kicking his leg out from under him and sending him down on one knee. She snatched up her gun.

She pointed the weapon at him and said, "Put your hands behind your head and don't move."

"I told you I'm with the Navy."

"So you say."

"Not the trusting type?"

"Not when some guy who claims to be with the Navy just had me pinned to the floor in an apartment that belongs to a man I need to question."

"Like hell!" he bellowed, still on bent knee as he turned toward her. "For what?"

"I don't have to explain anything to you."

"Can I rise?"

"As long as you keep your hands where I can see them."

A.J. straightened and let his hands fall loosely to his sides. His stance was completely deceptive and, to anyone else, he would probably look at ease and harmless, but Sienna had a keen eye. He looked like a man who could snap to attention in a second or take down an opponent even faster with deadly results.

"Can I get my ID out?"

"Two fingers," she cautioned.

He retrieved it and sure enough, it said he was Lieutenant A. J. Camacho, but Sienna wasn't going to let him off the hook that easily. Look what happened when she'd neglected to follow police procedure.

"I have every right to be here."

"That so?" She rubbed at her neck and he was instantly contrite.

"Sorry about that." He approached her and wasn't alarmed when she steadied the gun at him. He pushed it aside, lifting her fingers so he could see her flesh.

With his thumbs, he caressed the skin he'd abraded. "That's going to bruise. I'm really sorry about that."

Sienna stepped away from his disturbing touch. Admitting that he clearly wasn't a dangerous criminal, she holstered her gun. The steadiness of his gaze unnerved her, but Sienna drew a deep, uneven breath and made herself respond, her tone deliberately chastising. "Maybe some day I can return the favor."

He crossed his arms over his chest and gave her a cheeky off center grin. "I had no idea you were a woman, but I can sure see now how sadly mistaken I was."

Sienna looked up into his arresting eyes and took a deep breath. There was something about that smile that went straight to her heart. Damn, she'd always been a sucker for charmers. Her lot in life. "Sweet-talking me? Think that'll get you off the hook?"

Giving her a bad-boy grin, he said, "I can only throw myself on the mercy of the law."

"That would be the mercy of the court," Sienna corrected him and then sobered, trying to regain some of her professionalism. "What are you doing here?"

His gaze turned serious and repentant at the same time. "I'm looking for David...ah, Corporal Buckner."

"Is he AWOL?"

His brows lifted. "Unauthorized Leave—UL. The Navy doesn't use the AWOL acronym."

Sienna shrugged. Something about him sent warning bells to her brain. Danger, danger, danger. "Okay. Is he on unauthorized leave?"

"No." The distinct sound of hot wheels on asphalt was loud in the night. He looked away, went to the window and peeked out. "Looks like your backup is here."

She studied him, waiting for his answer. Something didn't jive here, but she wasn't sure what it was. "Then why would the navy be looking for him? Are you part of Naval Intelligence?"

"No."

"JAG?"

"Not quite."

"Then what right do you have to be here in this apartment and how did you get in?"

"I've got a key. I'm his stepbrother." He turned away from the window, careful to keep his hands in sight.

She'd been a detective long enough to know that people lied all the time about everything. She'd learned never to take anything at face value until she checked it out.

She pulled out a set of handcuffs. "Forgive me if I don't take your word for it."

"The cuffs aren't necessary."

"Yes, they are. I'm arresting you for assaulting a police officer. Everything else can be sorted out at the station."

A.J. nodded. He was smart, Sienna thought. It was prudent to acquiesce and save himself further trouble. He held out his hands.

"ARE YOU SAYING that the guy I handcuffed and brought in here really is David Buckner's stepbrother?"

"That's what I'm saying." Captain Raoul Sandoval was a dark, heavyset man whose parents had emigrated to the U.S. from Mexico. He smiled and sat gingerly on the edge of his desk. His dark eyes were sharp with a keen intelligence. Thick blue-black hair cut short gave him a military air and his bristly mustache always twitched when he was nervous or agitated. It was twitching now.

He held out a manila folder. "This information about Camacho was faxed from the navy. What they would release, anyway."

Sienna leaned back in the chair, bringing the file with her, dropping her head and closing her weary eyes.

"He's not Navy Intelligence, but..." Captain Sandoval began, indicating the file.

"There's a misnomer," Sienna said snidely and opened the folder. She sat bolt upright. "He's a SEAL. That explains it."

"Explains what?"

"They're the cowboys of the military."

"So?"

"Men like Camacho don't play by the rules. They

make up their own. It goes with being a SEAL. I don't like it when someone doesn't follow the rules.''

''He had every right to be there. The kid's his brother and he had a key. We have nothing to hold him on. We'll be lucky if he doesn't sue us for false arrest.''

She scowled at him. ''Serves him right for assaulting an officer.'' She rubbed at her neck and was sure there were marks. The guy didn't know his own strength.

She remembered the shock of meeting those intense eyes. Even now the memory made her feel uneasy and on the edge. He was a navy hotshot. So what. She could handle him. Handle? The unbidden thought of running her palms down the strong column of his chest made her shift uncomfortably in her seat.

''Sienna, apologize to the guy and let him go.''

''Apologize? I don't think I did anything wrong.'' Sienna sat forward and closed the file, placing it on his untidy desk.

Raoul followed her gaze and laughed at the annoyance on her face. Sienna stared back, arching her brow. He knew she didn't like clutter.

''Were you aware that a clean desk is the sign of a sick mind?'' he said.

Sienna smiled. ''I'd call that sour grapes, Captain.''

He smiled and then became serious. ''What's your progress on finding that truck full of guns?''

''I've sent the serial number of the M-16 we found

on the perp to the FBI. I canvassed the area where the perp said he took the gun, but perps lie all the time. I couldn't find anyone who saw anything. I was hoping to get a lead off Buckner.''

''What do you have on him?''

''Marine Corps Military Police, impeccable record, medals for heroism at the American Embassy in Angola during their civil war.''

''Yet?''

''Yet, an M-16 turns up on a perp who says he got the weapon from that area where Buckner's car is parked. I don't believe in coincidences. My gut instinct is that Buckner's involved somehow.''

''Did you contact the navy to see if any guns were reported missing?''

''Yes, but they denied that there was any truth to that. I asked them how they could explain the M-16 and they said that it could be part of someone's private collection.''

''Stay on top of this case, Parker. If there is a truckload of military weapons in this city and someone's selling them out of the back of a truck like ice-cream cones, I want that truck found and put out of commission.''

''Yes, sir.''

''As for Lieutenant Camacho, apologize. That's an order. Then get him out of here.''

Sienna rubbed at her throat, remembering how fast he moved. How strong his arm had been against her throat. She wasn't under any misconception that he would be a calm, easy-to-control type of guy. No, she wouldn't be able to run roughshod over him. Maybe that was why she was uneasy around him.

When she didn't move, Raoul looked directly at her. "What's the matter, Sienna, can't handle him?"

"I can handle any man, Captain, even the devil himself." That unbidden thought came again. How would his heavily muscled chest feel beneath her seeking hands?

Raoul laughed and slipped off the desk. "Good. Why don't you get moving and take the handcuffs off the guy?"

She went to leave his office.

"Oh, Parker, one more thing."

Sienna stopped with her hand on the doorknob. "Yes?"

"You're one of the most hardworking, sharp detectives in this department. No more overtime."

"Is that an order?" She arched her brow and gave him a cheeky grin.

"Get out of here."

While she walked back to her desk, she gathered her composure. She would remain professional. He was still sitting in the chair she'd placed him in. She dismissed the uniform cop she'd left guarding him.

A.J. looked up at her and her body reacted. She took a deep breath and grabbed his upper arm, trying not to drool over the hard thickness of his bicep. She turned him around and unlocked the cuffs, aware of every subtle shift of his big body.

"I guess I passed the test." He rubbed one wrist then the other.

"Yeah, but you don't get a gold star yet," she said as if talking to the village idiot. "I have to apologize to you. So, sorry."

"I can tell that was straight from your heart," he said.

Sienna watched his weathered hands in fascination. "Hey, I could have thrown you in a cell overnight instead of checking out your story right away."

She noticed his brow arch in reaction to the sudden anger that tinged her words.

"David's worth a night in jail," he said.

She heard the emotion in his voice and her world tilted, jeopardizing her safe, ordered life. Sympathy flooded her. "I only want to question him."

"Why?"

"Yesterday evening Tyrone Knight was stopped because he failed to yield to an emergency vehicle. He was found with an automatic weapon—an M-16. When I questioned him as to where he got the gun, he told me he took it from a truck parked in the warehouse district. He said there were a lot of weapons in the truck, including grenade launchers."

"That doesn't sound good. Did you contact the navy about any stolen weapons?"

"I'm working the case."

He put his hands up in surrender. "Got it. None of my business. So, what does this story have to do with my brother?"

"I went to the spot where the perp said he boosted the gun and I ran a check on a car I found in the area."

"I still don't see what this has to do with David."

"Does your brother own a red 1967 Mustang convertible?"

"Yeah."

"It was found in the same location as where the perp said the alleged truck was parked." With a cop's eyes, she watched A.J.'s reaction. If she expected to see something incriminating cross his face, she was disappointed. His face remained impassive.

"There could be any number of reasons why my brother's car was parked there."

She nodded slightly. "Agreed. I told you that I only wanted to question him. Does it alarm you that he's not home?"

A.J. shifted his stance and rubbed the back of his neck. "No," he said slowly. "David's very social and has a lot of friends. He's been known to spend a weekend or two with them."

"You have no idea where he could have gone?"

"No, but I'll contact my parents and see if they know where he is."

"What were you doing in his apartment?"

"I just got back from a mission and wanted to see if he'd like to get some dinner."

"What? No hot dates or big reunions on a Friday night?" she asked dryly.

A.J. cocked his hip, slipping one of his big hands into the pocket of his jeans. He peered at her from beneath his thick, dark lashes. "Do I detect a note of sympathy, Detective?"

"Nice try. That pleading, adorable, little-boy look is really good. Do women usually swoon about now?"

He laughed and stepped closer. "Where did you get all that beautiful red hair?"

The abrupt change in the discussion caught her totally off guard. Most men weren't able to do it. He'd done it twice in less than two hours. Sienna took a deep breath, knowing she should step back, but he smelled so good, and his voice was so seductive. When he reached out and captured one of her locks, she found that she couldn't quite swallow.

"So, spitfire. Where did you get this red, red hair?" He fingered the lock, the back of his knuckles grazing her cheekbone. His warm touch sent a buzzing sensation through her whole body.

Oh, no. It was rare, extremely rare. But there it was. A.J. Camacho was one of those men. *The kind she couldn't resist.* The air crackled, her breathing increased and she was sure her eyes were dilated. He turned her on just by taking up space. "I'll tell you if you tell me where you got your blue, blue eyes."

"My mom."

"Got my hair from the same place."

"My mom?"

He was cute, too. God help her. This time she was the one to laugh.

He leaned in and whispered in her ear. "Swooning yet?"

She was, but she wouldn't let him know it. "I'd prefer it if you addressed me as Detective Parker."

"Well, look at that, I outrank you."

"Too bad. I'm not in the military, remember?"

"Right." He stepped back. "So, where are we headed next?"

Sienna looked down at her watch and gasped. "I was supposed to be somewhere ten minutes ago." Adrenaline shot into her system at the disruption of her well thought out timetable. *Late* wasn't in her vocabulary. "I've got to go." She brushed past him, but he grabbed her arm and twisted her around.

He swung her a little too firmly and she came up hard against a very solid chest. For a moment she just blinked up at him. My God, the man was built.

"Whoa, there. You are quite a bundle of energy." He smiled at her with that bad-boy grin again. "I hate to bring this up, but my car is still at David's place and I have no ride. Since you're the one who dragged me over here…"

Sienna stepped away from him and eased her arm out of his grasp. "You're the one who assaulted an officer and caused me to be late. Take a cab. I'm meeting my friends at Enrique's. Buckner's apartment is in the wrong direction."

He shrugged those impossibly broad shoulders. "Enrique's is a great club. I can grab a cold one until you're finished."

"You're doing this to irritate me, aren't you?"

"You really are a detective," he said, a grin spreading across his face.

"Look, I have to swing by my apartment to change, and I would drop you at David's now, but that's across town." She could barely stand the fact that she was going to be late. She had to minimize where she could.

"These friends sound important to you."

"They are. We met last year on a case. I never miss my girls' night out." She bit her lip and came up with a final decision. "I could drop you by David's afterward, if that's okay with you," she suggested grudgingly.

"Thanks."

"I have to make a phone call. Wait out by the entrance."

"Sure." He walked away and Sienna couldn't help but notice how nicely the jeans he wore fit to his backside.

As Sienna called Lana Dempsey's cell phone, she

watched with appraising eyes as A. J. Camacho walked down the hall, past the bullpen and its rows of desks. He stopped at the front desk to converse amicably with the sergeant on duty as he waited for Sienna. Lana answered on the second ring, but Sienna couldn't take her eyes away from A.J. She quickly explained her lateness and told Lana she'd be there shortly.

SEALs were in hideously good shape, Sienna thought as she grabbed her purse from her desk. She'd bet a quarter would bounce off his butt. Sienna's eyes again strayed to that part of his anatomy, finely displayed as he leaned into the counter.

Sienna consciously unclenched her jaw, feeling a slight headache at her temples.

It wouldn't be any hardship rolling around on the mattress with him, Sienna thought. As she came up to him, she moved her eyes slowly up his body to the devastating dark intensity of his profile, her stomach flipping over as he smiled at something the desk sergeant said. With that disarming smile still on his face, he looked at her and Sienna sucked in her breath. Her whole body ignited and began to burn—again.

Some people have all the damn luck and she sure as hell wasn't one of them.

A dangerous man, A. J. Camacho. A deadly combination of looks, brains and courage. A risk if she ever saw one and Sienna wasn't into risk taking.

Yet, a deep, dark part of her could see herself engaging in a wild, passionate fling with him.

But, that was all.

This type of man *was* a lethal threat to her sanity and her perfectly structured life.

2

A.J. HAD TO ADMIT that the redhead was fine, with her dark green fiery eyes framed by pretty, sherry eyelashes, a soft, no-nonsense mouth, and a don't-mess-with-me attitude. He really liked her attitude. His father would have called her a tough broad.

A.J. would call her off-limits, except she looked like the type of woman who wouldn't care if he did. A woman who was this tough about her professional life would be as tough about her personal life, too. She wouldn't be looking for a temporary maverick. This kind of woman would be looking for permanence. It was something he sensed. Sienna Parker liked to call the shots and resented being out of the loop or out of control. He didn't have a problem with strong women.

He liked the way she moved—graceful, intense energy sizzling around her. Her tall, sexy body was curved in all the right places and that smooth cameo face framed by the tousled strands of red hair made him want to do something really stupid.

Even with her tough attitude the lady still looked like a lady. The tailored slacks and jacket in a soft

dove gray with tiny purple pinstripes was a far cry
from masculine. Nor did she try to hide that she was
a woman, for she'd complemented the suit with a soft
lilac blouse and a tiny silver heart around her creamy
throat. Her flaming red hair, although tamed and cut
shoulder-length was in a sexy style that looked like
she belonged on the pages of *Vogue*. Pretty loops with
etched flowers adorned her ears.

The result was a neatness that shouted she was a
professional, but still had the one-two punch of blaz-
ing sex.

Her personality was evident even now. She drove
the speed limit and didn't run yellow. A cop to the
core.

"What does A.J. stand for?" She stayed focused
on the road with a single-minded intensity that he
liked. Her eyes were always moving, checking out
everyone and everything. Just as he said, she was a
bundle of energy.

"Alejandro Jesus. My mother had a brother that
died fighting for freedom and so she thought that I
would be the perfect one to be his namesake." The
light up ahead of them turned yellow and Sienna
shifted slightly to apply the brake.

"Why did she think that?" She looked at him, her
eyes very dark in the dim interior of the car. The
bottom half of her face was illuminated by the light
from a street lamp. Her mouth was full, red and
looked enticing.

"I was the first child in my family to be born in America. The first one to be born free." He got a catch in his chest every time he said it out loud. The light turned green and she continued on her way.

"Ah." The look she gave him was knowing and all assessing.

"What's that supposed to mean?"

"Explains why you're in the navy. You want to protect that freedom."

For some strange reason her instant understanding of who he was made him hunger for more contact with her, reminding him of his loneliness of late. Too many missions and not enough time spent with people, especially women. "Pegged me in one, Sergeant. So what's your story?"

"What do you mean?"

Her tone was evasive and his honed senses wondered what she might want to conceal. "Why a cop?"

"I like the structure and the discipline."

"The desk sergeant said you were one of the youngest detectives on the force."

"I am. Were you checking up on me? Doubting my abilities?"

"I didn't have to say a word. I think he has a fatherly fondness for you. The guy got his back up."

Sienna shrugged. "What did you do to get his back up?"

"It might have been the simple question I asked."

"What was the question?"

"I asked him if you were attached."

"You did?" She stopped a little too hard at the stop sign. Another traffic rule she took completely at face value. No rolling stops for this woman.

"What did he say?" She turned large green eyes to him.

"He said no and that I shouldn't get any bright ideas in that area if my intentions weren't honorable."

"What did you say?"

"I asked him if he was your father."

"So, are your intentions honorable?"

His eyes traveled from the top of her head to the tips of her toes. "No."

"Thanks for the warning."

"You're pretty cool under fire."

"I have the feeling you are, too."

"Steady as a rock."

"So nothing can shake you?"

"Depends."

"On what?"

"On the circumstances." She had squared him up pretty good. SEAL training was the toughest around and it had prepared him well for combat. He'd always maintained his cool under fire. A SEAL once told him that some guys get that way. They see everything clearly and know exactly what to do. The guy had called him a born leader.

It didn't take long after she parked her car in the underground garage to get up the elevator to her apartment. She poured him a glass of iced tea and disappeared into her room. A.J. looked out her window admiring her sweet view of the bay.

He loved the water and, in fact, his nickname during Basic Underwater Demolition/SEAL training or BUD/S had been Shamu. The water was like another world to him, quiet, shielding and familiar. During his training, he had won the record for holding his breath the longest underwater.

But when he heard Sienna come out of her bedroom and he turned, the fact that he could hold his breath the longest kept him from passing out. She was bending over slightly to slip on a strappy gold sandal. His eyes went up her exquisite body, all five feet seven inches of her. The tight, sleeveless jade green microdress fit her like a second skin, the hem of the dress hitting her at the top of her well-toned, mouth-watering thighs. He wondered about what he couldn't see. What kind of streamlined underwear could be so seamless? His mouth went dry at the thought. Her hair blazed on top of her head where she'd pinned it up, but it was a gorgeous haphazard free fall and tumbled in untidy tendrils to her nape, her throat and around her delicate face.

She looked voluptuous and wild and sexual and she looked—ah, man, she looked…

Off-limits, he thought, finally taking a deep breath to feed his oxygen-starved brain. Yet it wasn't his brain that was paying attention to Sienna Parker.

She looked up then, after checking the tiny buckle on the sandal, her face perplexed. "What's wrong?"

"Remember when I said that I don't shake easily?"

Her face scrunched up and then cleared. "Right, depends on the circumstances."

"This is one of those circumstances."

She walked gracefully up to him on those heels. "What are you talking about?"

He realized that he was babbling.

He picked up her hand and very gently kissed her palm. "I'm shaking."

HER PALM STILL TINGLED from his mouth, a full, sensual mouth that had captured all of Sienna's attention. She was angry with herself for letting his incredible charm seduce her, but the man oozed sex appeal. Any woman would be affected, so it must be okay to be a little dazzled.

Except she didn't want to be dazzled. Hadn't she promised herself that she wouldn't cross over the bridge from San Diego to Coronado to club? The navy men were either intense warriors or arrogant jerks. She wanted safe and comfortable men who stayed home on the weekends.

Besides, traveling from port to port didn't interest her. Oh no, that was not for her. She liked San Diego, a city she knew. She liked being a cop and it was another reason to stay away from navy types. She couldn't build a career if she was constantly moving.

They entered the glass elevator that would take them on a scenic ride to the top of the high-rise where the club was located.

When Sienna walked into the club, the music was pumping and people were on the dance floor gyrating to the beat. Both Lana Dempsey and Kate Quinn were already sitting at their usual table. Sienna could feel their eyes following them the moment they entered the club even though she was across the room in the bar area. She left A.J. with a quick goodbye. Sienna sat down heavily.

"I can see why you were late. Yowza! Who's Mr. Yummy?" Lana asked, taking a sip of her drink. Lana had delicate cheekbones and a full mouth. Her long, dark hair and a smile that lit up a room gave her an ethereal, fragile quality, but Sienna knew Lana was tough. She was one of the few women firefighters that San Diego employed. Not only could she carry one hundred pounds on her shoulders down ten flights of stairs, she was a certified EMT, had her diving license, and possessed so many other certifications Sienna had lost track of them.

"Just a guy I happened to mistakenly think was a burglar. I arrested him." Great, now she'd have to talk about him when she was supposed to be relaxing. Lana was a pit bull when she got her perfect white teeth into something.

"Wow. Nice eye candy." Lana popped a pretzel in her mouth, without removing her gaze from A.J.

"Lana, stop staring. He's a navy tough guy with a brother I've got to question. He needs a ride back to where I picked him up."

"He's navy? Have you seen him in his whites? A guy is so sexy in uniform. You should see Sean when he puts on his blues," Lana said, searching through the snack mix in the bowl on the table until she found another pretzel, then she dropped it into her mouth. Every other word out of Lana's mouth was about Sean O'Neill. Sienna wished she would just admit she wanted to date the guy and get on with it.

Sienna gave Lana a withering look. "No. I just met him today."

Lana smiled and lobbed a pretzel at Sienna. "So, consider it your lucky day. How long has it been, Sienna?"

"Too long," Sienna exhaled heavily. "But, I promised myself no navy guys."

"Why not? It's wham-bam-thank-you-sir." Lana snickered. "It's no big deal. He's hot!"

"A SEAL is too adventurous for my taste."

"And six feet two inches of hard-packed muscle, devastating Latino looks and great eyes. Sounds like a terrible hardship."

"He does fit the profile for a hot fling, but I have so much work to do."

"For Pete's sake, Sienna, take a freakin' chance.

It's not like you have to marry the guy. Stop doing everything by the book and break some rules."

"Look who's talking. Lana, you know all about dangerous, forbidden relationships. You've been drooling over that co-worker of yours since I met you and you've done nothing about him." The words were coming out of her mouth before she had a chance to engage her brain. She would never bait her friend this way, but Lana's dare to go after A.J. made Sienna nervous and oversensitive. Sienna couldn't help but lash out. There were so many emotions just beneath her skin, emotions she had no intention of acknowledging.

It didn't help that A.J. scared her to death way deep down inside. He had easily gotten beyond the first barrier she put up against men like him. And she was petrified to let him have a crack at any of her other barriers, to open herself up to the kind of hurt he was sure to bring her. Two people could not be more different than they were. He was adventurous and she was as conservative as they came.

"Are you challenging me to go after Sean?" Lana said, raising her brows and effectively breaking into Sienna's thoughts.

Oh, no…Sienna knew that look. "No, Lana…" Sienna said.

"You think I'm afraid of him sexually?" Lana bit her lip and studied Sienna's face. "You don't think I'll take this dare? Do you?"

"I didn't say that. Can't we just relax, have a drink and listen to the music?"

Lana's eyes were sparking with anger. "You think I can't seduce Sean."

Oh, great. Sienna knew from experience that Lana wouldn't let this drop until she'd proven herself. Sienna tried to diffuse the situation, her tone conciliatory, "I think you're intimidated by the fact that you work together and it could mess up your friendship. It's a legitimate concern, Lana."

"I'll do it if you go after this SEAL," she shot back.

"How did I get drawn into this conversation?" Sienna said shaking her head.

"I bet with a body like that he knows a tremendous amount about how to make a woman scream," Kate offered.

With shock coursing through her, Sienna turned to Kate. Her demure friend was always a lady, always prim and proper. Because of it she and Lana called her Sister Kate. Lana, who had been about to retort, closed her mouth with a snap, her eyes riveting on Kate.

"Sister Kate, have you been reading *Cosmo*?" Lana asked.

"No. I dare you to get the SEAL in bed, Sienna and you to get Sean, Lana." Kate picked up a peanut and ate it.

"Not you, too, Kate?" Sienna moaned. Who would

have believed it? Kate looked like an angel with her sweet, soft face, big doe eyes and long, curly blond hair. "Are you out of your mind? Why would I want to do that?"

"Because you need a life. You work too hard and are too much of a good little cop," Lana said, giving Kate a wicked look. "That accountant you dated for six months only wanted to do it in the missionary position. Talk about boring. Besides, you think the SEAL's hot. You've checked him out about six times since you sat down."

"I have not!" Sienna rubbed at her face with both hands.

"Methinks the lady doth protest too much," Lana said, giving Sienna an I-think-you're-lying look.

"It would be stupid and reckless." Sienna bit her lip. "But I have to admit that I want to take him to bed."

"That's the fighting spirit!" Lana crowed.

"I for one am tired of being so good all the time," Kate said.

Sienna and Lana both looked at her.

Pit bull Lana smiled and Sienna knew Lana had a new target. "Jericho St. James."

"San Diego's premiere assistant district attorney?" Sienna asked.

"Yup."

"Lana, Kate would never engage in a hot, sweaty affair. She's a straitlaced scientist, for heaven's sake.

Would you, Kate?'' Sienna looked at Kate and knew she'd missed something. "Okay, what did I miss?"

"I had to testify in court today and when he cross-examined me, he couldn't seem to take his eyes off my legs."

"And…?'' Sienna prompted.

"You should see that man give a summation to the jury. My God, the passion in him is palpable." Kate fanned herself. "He's quite gorgeous."

"If you want to, accept the dare, Kate. Go after him," Lana challenged.

"There's just one problem. He is intimidating and a bit…forceful." Kate said as she looked from Lana to Sienna.

"Sister Kate, you *have* been reading *Cosmo,* but you're not following the advice," Lana admonished.

"I'm sick of you two calling me Sister Kate all the time."

"So how are you going to get close to Jericho St. James?" Lana asked, sitting forward, knowing that she'd won. Kate was hooked.

"Well, as a matter of fact, after the trial he told me he wanted to make arrangements to see me. He had an important matter to discuss."

"So make your move then?"

"What? In his office or in the lab?"

Lana made clucking noises.

"I am not chicken!"

"Kate, he's a gorgeous, high-profile ADA," Lana said.

"Right and I'm a forensic pathologist in a white coat that provides him with DNA evidence so he can go to trial."

"You're changing the subject. Who cares what you do for a living? Sex with Jericho is on the table, take it or be Sister Kate for the rest of your life."

"I'll take it."

"We need to toast that." They clinked their glasses.

"So," Kate said, "I'll go after Jericho, Lana is going after Sean, and you're going after hunky what's his name?"

"A. J. Camacho."

"A. J. Camacho. So the chase is on, ladies."

"I think we need to prove that we slept with the guy," Lana said, taking another sip of her drink.

"The burden of proof is on each of us. Concrete evidence will be required," Kate agreed.

Sienna asked, "Evidence? What do you mean? Like a pair of undies or something?" This seemed to be getting out of control.

"Sure. An article that shows you slept with the guy," Kate confirmed.

Lana laughed out loud and clapped her hands. "This from a forensic pathologist. It doesn't surprise me. This is great. We are women who dare!"

"And we have until we all collect our souvenirs?" Sienna asked.

"That's right," Kate agreed.

Sienna looked over at A.J. Could she really do this? He didn't fit into her orderly world.

A SEAL would be the kind of man who would challenge her to step out of her safe existence. So, A.J. was not long-term, but with his hard body and devastating looks, she knew the short-term would mean hot, earth-shattering sex.

From where he was sitting at the L-shaped bar, she could see he was talking to the bartender and smiling. Damn, what a smile. On the swoon meter, Sienna would give him an eleven, maybe even a twelve. While she watched him, he pushed his hair back with a graceful gesture that caused his right arm to ripple. Sienna's knees went weak. Okay, he was off the meter. As if he could feel her watching him, he looked directly into her eyes.

A.J. FELT THE FULL impact of those enticing green eyes. The pull from across the bar was magnetic. She smiled and got up. Could he hope she was coming over here to talk to him? No, he told his traitorous body. He shouldn't be hoping at all.

She stopped at his bar stool. "Would you like to dance, sailor?"

A.J. smiled and slid off the barstool. "The pleasure would be all mine, Sergeant."

The dance floor was awash in a soft golden light and so crowded that Sienna was pressed to A.J. as soon as he took her in his arms.

She knew he was asking her a question, but she couldn't take her eyes off his mouth. The urge to kiss him washed over her in waves, and she wondered who was seducing whom.

"What?"

"Do you like this song?" he repeated—this time into her ear and she shivered from the close contact.

"Yes," she said above the strains of the music, her eyes focusing on his mouth again.

"You have amazing eyes," he murmured, his mouth still close to the delicate shell of her ear.

"Thanks." *He* had such a beautiful mouth.

He jerked slightly when her thumb traced over the fullness of his bottom lip.

When she looked up into his eyes, she got the most incredible sensation, like a hot and cold prickly feeling that radiated throughout her whole body. Those eyes. Blue like the color of true, heartbreaking sapphires. They were startling.

Wild eyes. Eyes that promised surprises; that mesmerized with energy, with the wicked wit that lurked behind them. Eyes that made her wary, that taunted her like a peek into a forbidden room. Eyes that should have belonged to the devil himself.

He tilted his head and she tracked the movement

with her gaze. Softly he said, "What are you waiting for?"

She made a small sound in her throat, almost a protest, before her arms encircled his neck and drew him closer. She fused her mouth to his and felt as if she were sliding down a hot, slick slope. Holy cow. Hot damn. She was lost, immediately and completely, and it'd never happened to her before. She only realized now that this is what she'd wanted to do since she'd taken the cuffs off him at division headquarters.

His mouth was incredibly soft, incredibly hot…just incredible.

The kiss was carnal, long and fierce and Sienna was suddenly dazed when A.J. pulled away.

"You pack a punch, Sergeant."

"Sienna."

He smiled. "A.J."

She rested her chin on his shoulder and became aware of Lana and Kate each giving her an enthusiastic thumbs-up. Sienna rolled her eyes and waved them off.

He leaned down again and whispered in her ear. "Are you done with your friends?"

"Yes."

"Do you think you could take me back to David's now?"

Sienna's stomach jumped and she was about to utter something suggestive and wildly decadent when he again spoke.

"It's been a long day and I'm really tired."

Boy, he sure knew how to deflate a situation. She pulled away from him and swallowed. "Let me get my purse and say goodbye. Come over and meet my friends."

Sienna led him over to the table where both friends had broad grins on their faces. Sienna wanted to tell them that she'd struck out.

"Lana and Kate, meet Lieutenant A. J. Camacho."

Lana offered her hand and then Kate offered hers. He shook them both with a bemused look on his face. "With such a beautiful trio of women, it's hard to believe you would have a Friday night free."

Sienna was disgusted with the way they flushed and smiled, totally taken with A.J.

"We're heading out," Sienna said and Lana gave her a way-to-go look and pantomimed a phone to her ear when A.J. turned to leave. Sienna nodded and followed his broad back out of the bar.

In the elevator she started to stew about how easy it had been for him to dismiss her in the bar. She wondered if she was maybe losing her touch. She could have sworn he was attracted to her. The kiss was...

She slapped her hand against the stop button, jerking the elevator to a standstill. "Are my signals *really* bad or are you just not interested? And if so, why not?"

He stared at her a moment, then ran his hand

through his hair. God, didn't he know that didn't help?

She stepped closer to him. "Don't you like me, A.J.?"

"Yes, Sienna, I like you. I want you. I just can't offer much in terms of a relationship."

"Who asked you for that?"

"Well, no one, but I have a hunch that I'm not exactly your type."

"You're just like Captain Kirk."

"Pardon me?"

"Married to Star Fleet. Captain Kirk."

"Right, exactly. I'm dedicated to the navy."

"So you didn't like kissing me and you don't want to make hot, passionate love to me?"

"Whoa, slow this boat down. I never said that."

"So you liked kissing me?"

"Yeah. I really liked kissing you."

"Prove it."

It happened so fast that Sienna gasped. She'd forgotten how quick the man could move when she found herself pinned between the cool elevator wall and a hard, hot body.

His mouth slanted over hers. She sighed against it, even as the wet heat of his tongue came up against her parted lips, which she opened eagerly. She moaned as his tongue explored her mouth, possessively, expertly, running it along the silky sweetness, then capturing it, entwining it with his, stroking, tasting, leaving her begging for more, much more. His scent was intoxicating, very masculine, very seductive.

Sienna slid her hands up his strong arms and tangled her fingers in the longer hair at his nape. She had never realized how much passion she had inside her until she'd kissed this man. Now nothing short of having him inside her would be enough.

He pushed his hips against hers while he softened the impassioned kiss.

It was Sienna's undoing when his mouth moved over hers in such obvious worship like a man paying homage to something beyond his comprehension, something enchanting and captivating that it defied human understanding. She felt the heat of his arousal and moved against him with an abandon that startled her.

All Sienna's thoughts broke apart like glass shattering into tiny crystal shards.

He devoured her as if she were so sweet he couldn't get enough. Sienna all but cried out as he slipped his hands under her dress.

"I have to know," he said softly.

"Know what?" she panted back.

"What you have on under this dress."

She felt his hands on her outer thigh, over her hip, cupping her buttock in his hand and squeezing. He moved up to her waist and when he touched the silk, he sighed.

"A thong. That's it?"

"Just my skin."

He ran his hand around the silk band until he reached her nest of curls. "Damn Sienna, you've made me lose control."

The heat in his eyes was more than lust. It was more powerful, more pure—almost transcendental, making the blue of his eyes seem luminous and soft. She blinked a couple of times, but then lost her train of thought when A.J. slid his hand over her mound.

"Wet," he said, slipping a finger inside her.

"I heard SEALs liked getting wet."

"We love it."

His mouth came down on hers as he rubbed at her nerve-rich center. The sensation built between her legs, their mouths twisted passionately, lips fierce, tongues wildly mating.

"You're so tight, so wet," he murmured, his hand coming up to cup her breast through the tight material. He bent his head and took her into his mouth, biting gently on her distended nipple through the fabric. It was the most amazing feeling to be fully clothed and be ravished at the same time.

"A.J.," she said raggedly, the hard sensations in her groin narrowing down to a tight, aching need. His mouth came back up to hers.

Sienna shuddered and the ball of sensations inside her exploded as she came apart in his arms.

Even as the contractions of her climax receded, he

turned her body until she was facing the glass. The city was a glow around them, the glass-enclosed tube too far up for anyone to see them. It was like making love among the stars.

Before she could catch her breath, he jerked up her dress to her waist. She arched into the thick heat of him as he pressed his cock against her.

He groaned when she spread her legs and eagerly slid his fingers into the moisture there. He groaned again, pinning her against the glass. She heard a foil packet rip and with one swift lunge, he entered her. The glorious friction as he slid in and out of her in quick succession made her press her hands hard to the glass, her vision a haze of sparkling images, the streetlights, the bright buildings below and the hard, twinkling stars. He thrust deeper and harder; his steely arm went around her waist holding her tightly.

His free hand gripped the bodice of her stretchy dress and pulled it down. His fingers found her nipple and he twisted it between his fingers, causing sharp sensations from her breast to her groin.

That pushed her over the top. She pressed back and with a sharp cry, came—an endless shivering cascade of sensation, more intense than any orgasm she had ever experienced.

After a moment of catching her breath and rearranging her clothes, her gaze clashed with A.J.'s.

He smiled slow and easy. "How does it feel to break the law?"

"What?"

"Indecency in public. Against the law."

She smiled back. "We're not in public."

"Ah, a technicality." He cupped her cheek. "How about you take me to my car and follow me home? We can explore other ways to break the law."

Down in the car, she started up the engine. She was eager for a night of hot sex with him, so much so that she found herself speeding. She released her foot from the gas and resumed a more sedate pace.

But the closer she got to David's apartment, the more she couldn't stop thinking about it and the more she wanted his delicious mouth and body again. When they pulled up outside, she didn't get a moment to say a word to him.

Her beeper went off. For a split second, she thought about not answering it. Appalled at her reaction, common sense reasserted itself as she realized that she couldn't. She used her cell phone to call division HQ and found out that one of her ongoing cases had blown wide-open.

After hanging up, she looked at him. "I'm sorry."

He leaned over the seat and gave her a hard kiss on the mouth and she almost changed her mind again.

"So am I," he whispered. Then he was out of the car and inside his.

She sat for a moment in dismay, until the taillights of his car disappeared around a corner.

She wanted to follow him and… What was the matter with her? she asked herself as she sat in her dark car. Uneasiness twined through her like thorns around a trellis, painful and tight. Maybe she'd been too hasty in taking the dare from her friends.

Haste made waste wasn't just a saying for nothing.

Instead of following A.J., like she'd really wanted to only moments before, she turned her car around and headed in the opposite direction.

3

SIENNA'S GLOVED fist hit the bag. It was smart to let A.J. disappear into the night. Her misgivings about sleeping with him again were as strong this Monday morning as they were on Friday night.

Working through the weekend hadn't diffused the impact of the kiss they'd shared or the tingling she experienced when she remembered him pressed against her while they danced. So, it was no surprise that she could envision A.J.'s heavy, naked body covering hers. Easy answer. He was smooth, hot and good in bed. Who was she kidding? He was great in bed.

This morning she realized she should have kept a level head when her daring girlfriends had come up with the souvenir-gathering escapade. She'd escaped that temptation—just barely. Now it was too late to worry about getting anything at all from A.J. And she had no intention of seeking him out, not when the urge to take him was so strong in her.

Sienna accepted that. There was no use in mulling over decisions made, even ones made in the heat of the moment.

In fact, it would have been easy to forget about A.J. if only he hadn't been so amazing otherwise. *Funny* and *intelligent* were words that easily came to her mind as she executed a couple of wicked right hooks along with a couple of undercuts. Dancing around the bag, she lifted her leg, the hard toned muscle contracting as it whipped out at the bag.

The San Diego police gym was nearly deserted as most of the patrol cops had reported for roll call. Sienna glanced around the large rectangular structure that had been built to accommodate officers who needed to hone their bodies to tackle the everyday job of taking down perps. But all the weight machines stood idle, the thick mats on the floor empty and the showers quiet.

She liked the early morning hours when she monopolized the gym. The silence was soothing. A balm before the ugliness of the world intruded on her, a time to be alone with her thoughts.

There were a lot of pressing things to think about. The case that had blown wide open ended with one of the biggest drug dealers in the city behind bars. The arrest had put a feather in Sienna's cap, but shutting down his business meant more to her than the prestige. One more bit of slime off the streets.

Not to mention the fact that in all the activity with the drug squad, Sienna had missed another fitting for her sister's wedding. With it happening this weekend, she was running out of time.

Something tugged on Sienna's heart. Something she wouldn't name or acknowledge. She felt in awe that her sister had the kind of courage to embrace love without fear. Michelle had always been the type of person who fit in and made friends easily.

Not the same for Sienna. She'd always been apart, no matter how hard her foster parents, Lynne and Scott, had tried to pull her into their family. Sienna had played it safe and kept her heart sheltered.

"If you hit that bag any harder, you'll rip it open."

The sound of Lana's voice made Sienna smile. "What are you doing here? Isn't it bleacher day? Your leg muscles will get flabby."

"Naw. That's tomorrow."

Sienna turned to see Lana walking across the deserted gym. She was dressed in the same attire as Sienna, a black sports bra and tight Lycra shorts. Her long dark hair was tied into a ponytail.

"Don't you firefighters have your own facility?" Sienna said with a teasing tone.

"Sure we do. But you know how much I *love* to sweat with you."

When she reached Sienna, she took hold of the bag. "How did it go Friday night with the SEAL?"

"You were right, he's good and Kate knew what she was talking about. He made me scream," Sienna growled and hit the bag.

Lana's eyebrows rose, a knowing look in her eyes. "All night I hope."

"No, I got a call from headquarters and had to work."

"God, Sienna."

"I had a hot fling with the guy, in the elevator no less, so ease up. I was almost naked in public."

Lana laughed. "Well, that's something."

"Hey, there's a lot more to A.J. than just his body." Sienna huffed out a breath, striking the bag with a front kick that drove Lana a few inches backward. Sienna followed with a quick series of jabs. "A whole lot of dangerous stuff. Sex is easy, Lana, and this thing with A.J. has *complicated* written all over it."

"He's a SEAL. They're gone usually. I'm sure he won't bother you much."

He's bothering me all the time, Sienna thought. She imagined him sprawled on a bed waiting for her. All that sleek, hot muscle on display, lying there hard and ready for her. She remembered his eyes, alive with a personality that drew her almost beyond her will to resist. "I hope not. He's not someone who would be right for me."

"You know this after one encounter with him?" Lana said, bracing herself as Sienna took a few more hard swings at the bag.

"I know he's unconventional and that irks me." She slammed her fist into the bag so hard she felt the vibration up her arm.

"That's because you're a control freak," Lana said matter of factly and smiled.

"It takes one to know one," Sienna countered.

Lana shrugged. "I don't deny that I'm a control freak. I think as public servants there's a lot of pressure on us and we don't want to fail. Because our failure affects real lives."

"Your father still putting pressure on you to make captain?"

"Nothing changes there. He's been telling me that since I was old enough to understand. Don't change the subject. I think we want to control the situation, you with criminals and me with fire."

Sienna dropped her arms, suddenly feeling the fatigue in them from the constant punching. Her thighs were screaming from the intense kicking.

"What else is bothering you?"

"Nothing."

Lana gave her a look full of skepticism. "Come on, Sienna." When Sienna remained quiet, Lana let go of the bag and put her hands on her hips. "You are so stubborn. Before my sister's arson and FBI problems, you refused to go clubbing with Kate and me because you were working most of the time. What made you change your mind?"

Sienna suddenly felt herself struggling with a thick wad of emotion. How could she explain? It was always so hard for her to make connections. "You saved my life, Lana, when you pushed me out from under that burning beam.'' She'd never forget how all three of them met. Paige Dempsey, Lana's sister, had her warehouse torched and was implicated on a fraud issue, involving her soon-to-be husband, FBI agent Justin Connor.

It wasn't until Kate had come to Sienna to ask her to help them clear Paige's name that Sienna had let the two women into her life. She hadn't regretted one moment with them.

''You never said anything about it.''

''I know and I should have. It's just that…well, I really didn't know what friendship was until I met you two.''

''Hell, me and Sister Kate really like you, too.''

''Ha, Sister Kate. She wasn't so timid when I was reprimanded on that arson case to clear your sister.'' A warmth settled in Sienna's heart as she remembered how Kate had bristled at Captain Sandoval and went toe to toe with him on her behalf. It was the first time in Sienna's life that she could remember someone standing up for her, someone who had nothing to gain at all.

Sienna looked at Lana, then away. Even though she'd known these two women for a year and she had confided in them, she really hadn't told them how much they meant to her. Lana and Kate had stood by her then and had continued to stand by her ever since. She owed them—they brought laughter and camaraderie into her life. Suddenly, she couldn't seem to be quiet. "Kate was like a protective pit bull. We were a team during that investigation and I need you two." The declaration made Lana smile, and she hugged Sienna for a quick, brief moment.

"Kate was awesome. The both of you were awesome. Thanks to you two, Paige was cleared," Lana said, grabbing at the bag to stop the swinging motion.

"Have Paige and Justin set the date?" Sienna asked.

"No, not yet, but they're working on it." Lana stepped forward. "I'm glad you told me all this."

Sienna nodded and met Lana's gaze. She hit the bag hard. "I find it difficult to confide in other people. I was alone a lot when I was young, before the Thompsons took me in."

"By design?"

"Yes."

"Friends are there for each other and Kate and I need you in our lives, too. So stop sandbagging me and tell me what else is bothering you."

Sienna felt a twinge of reluctance. The thought of opening herself to the gutsy firefighter made her stomach churn. She took a deep breath and said, "I missed another fitting."

Lana let go of a breath. "It shouldn't be a problem, unless you're doing it on purpose."

Sienna hit the bag with a combination of vicious hooks and jabs. Her voice shook with the exertion.

"I really want to be in her wedding. Even though we're seven years apart, we're pretty close.

"Isn't it the third time you've missed it? If I'm not mistaken, the wedding is this weekend."

"I warned her that it would be hard for me to plan anything. Cops' hours weren't normal."

"Are you going to reschedule?" Lana asked gently.

"As soon as I can."

"Parker!"

It was her captain's voice and for a moment she was disoriented. She looked up at the clock on the wall and saw that she still had an hour before reporting for duty.

"This looks really official. I should go, but call me if you want to talk," Lana said, laying her hand on Sienna's arm. "Anytime you want to talk." She turned and headed out of the gym.

Sienna gave the bag one last punch, turned around and came face to face with Lieutenant A. J. Camacho dressed officially in his pristine white uniform. He was shaved, impeccably groomed and had his hat tucked under his arm.

In that uniform, A.J. glowed with fierce masculinity, so much so that she was sure she wasn't the first woman to go all doe-eyed when she saw him. Her reaction to him was too intense, out of all proportion. It shook her to the core. And the last thing she needed now was a man who drove her crazy. So crazy, she couldn't think straight.

Caught off guard at his presence, Sienna tensed. Her eyes narrowed and focused on him while every muscle in his body tightened as he became alert. It was a heightened instinctual response to danger and she wasn't sure he was even aware of it.

It bothered her that she should react to him this way and she took a confrontational stance, spurred on by his official dress. "I feel like I should salute."

"Gauging by the look on your face, I'd say it'd be the one-finger kind." He smiled and tilted his head slightly, watching her like a sleek panther mildly intrigued by a mouse.

And she had no doubt at all that he was as dangerous as that panther and the fact that he thought her as ineffectual as a mouse irritated her, too.

She smiled back sweetly, but her eyes were hard. "No doubt. Did you forget to tell me something when you were here Friday?"

"He's working with you."

The words registered, but they hadn't come from A.J. Her captain was still standing nearby. "What?" she asked, dazed. "Did I hear you right?"

"Nothing wrong with your hearing, Parker."

"Why, exactly?" She looked at her captain in frustration. How could he saddle her with the very man Sienna wanted to be miles away from?

"He's being assigned to us to work this gun case

with you. The navy doesn't want all those weapons floating around on the streets, either. He's your special liaison purely in an official capacity,'' Raoul said.

"I can handle this case without the U.S. Navy breathing down my neck.''

"I have complete confidence in you, Parker. But this comes from the mayor. He wants those assault weapons off the street. We have no choice. It's now a joint investigation.'' She could see the apology and the sympathy in his eyes, but it did nothing to alleviate the building anger.

Captain Sandoval turned and left, the gym door closing on the seething silence.

She glared at him. With a one-word epithet, she pulled off the boxing gloves and with deliberate precision threw each one at him. He fended off each glove automatically.

Then she marched past him intending to take a long shower. Maybe the hot water would help her deal with the fact that the man whom she couldn't resist and hoped to never see again was going to be tagging her practically 24/7. Short of committing professional suicide by refusing to work with him, she had to suck it up and bite her tongue.

"Sienna, wait.''

He grabbed her arm. Cold fear and expectant heat both washed through her. Fear of herself and the unaccustomed intensity of her desires; heat because where this man was concerned, she couldn't seem to control that desire.

He drew her toward him. "Hands off, hotshot."

He flashed her a look petulant and dangerous. Too much like Lucifer brooding on some secret fantasy of rebellion. "You didn't have any problem with me Friday night."

Something in Sienna snapped. She pivoted, twisted out of his grasp, and took him down to the mat. Following him down, she pressed her knee into his sternum.

His hat flew from his grasp and the air woofed out of his lungs with a satisfying sound. A.J. looked up at her and spread his arms, his palms up as if her anger was a palpable thing he had to ward off.

"Whoa, Sienna," he gasped.

"I don't like to be *ambushed,* Lieutenant."

"Can I explain or are you going to teach me a lesson?"

"Are you mocking me?" She glared at him, pressing her knee a little deeper into his hard flesh. Remembering how his sleek belly and hard muscled thighs had felt against her skin.

"Hell, no. I believe you could do it." He rested his head and shoulders against the mat to release some of the pressure against his chest.

"Explain why you're really here," she ordered tightly.

"You told me yourself that my brother could be implicated in a theft of guns."

"You went behind my back, mister."

"Yes," he said emphatically, "I did."

A.J. took a deep breath. Sienna could feel the movement of his hard body beneath hers and for a moment she got lost in the sensation.

"If you think that I'm going to wait around and do nothing when David may be in danger, you're crazy. I had my stepfather, Senator Anthony Buckner call the Secretary of the Navy, who called the mayor, who called the commissioner, who called your captain."

"It's not like your brother's a suspect. He may have information that could help my investigation." She paused. "Why don't you just call him and have him come down to division HQ? I can hear what he has to say and you can go on your merry way."

"I would if I could, but he's missing." He watched her as the words sank in, a solemn expression darkening his eyes.

She released all the pressure on his chest, her heart lurching.

"My stepfather and mother are frantic. My brother's commanding officer called. He's officially UL."

"But I thought you said he wasn't UL on Friday." She removed her leg and got off him. Standing, she offered him her hand.

"On Friday he wasn't, but he didn't report for duty

on Saturday." He looked at her hand warily, but then placed his in hers. With his help, she hauled him to his feet.

Having complete control over him on the mat was preferable to standing in front of him. He was taller than her and made her feel every inch the woman. Sienna explained, "You and I both know that coincidences rarely happen. I was very eager to talk to your brother because he was parked in that area and he's in the military. It seemed to me that there was a good chance he's somehow involved."

"So Friday you were using your calm, cool, I-just-want-to-question him tone to keep me from being alarmed."

He ran his hand through his hair and for the first time, Sienna saw the worry before he masked it. She wanted to console him. She had the overpowering urge to touch him but refrained. "I've read your brother's file. He's a model Marine. Doesn't seem like the type who'd be involved in stolen weapons."

"He'd die before he'd betray the Corps. He wouldn't ever worry my mother, unless..." He trailed off, this time unable to hide the worry in his eyes.

Sienna finished for him. "He was unable to call."

"Right."

Sienna took a cleansing breath, stubbornly holding on to a little bit of her anger. "I don't like it when you go behind my back. Okay."

"I won't apologize for trying to help my brother and I'll do it any way I can."

"Just stick to the rules from now on and we won't have any friction." Sienna turned away from the sheer magnetism of the man and walked over to pick up her boxing gloves.

"Rules and regulations can hamper your thinking. Sometimes you have to think outside the box," he said softly, coming to stand behind her.

He was going to be difficult and troublesome. There was no getting around it. She turned and poked him in the chest. "Let's get one thing straight between us. On this investigation, it's my way. There will be no hotdogging. You will follow my lead."

He studied her with an unnerving, assessing look, as if he were seeing something no one else could see. Sienna swallowed and released his gaze, an unsettling flutter of awareness unfolding in her chest. Never back down, her brain was telling her. Let him know who's the boss. But for the first time in her life she tried to retreat. He crowded her.

"I did a pretty good job of following your lead last time we were together," A.J. intoned, his voice a husky rasp.

He was still watching her with a smile on his face, but it was an odd, distracted smile, as if his thoughts were focused on something else. Faltering under his intense scrutiny, she backed toward the gym exit that would lead her to the showers and safety.

A shiver ran down the full length of her spine. "Now that you've shoved your way into this case, it wouldn't be smart to engage in any…"

Sienna didn't realize that she was close to the exit until her back hit the wall.

He held her gaze, the glimmer in his devastating blue eyes intensifying. "Hot sex?"

"Exactly. I didn't really expect to see you again." She had nowhere else to go and A.J. pressed against the length of her body.

"But you wanted to."

"Yes, I did," she said, reluctantly.

"So why let a good thing go to waste? You know where I stand. I'm a navy man through and through. And you…" He hesitated.

"I'm what?" she asked warily.

His eyes dropped to her mouth and Sienna's heart did a full gainer with a twist. "You want to stay in your safe little world, but you got a taste of what it's like to step outside those barriers, and you liked it. Didn't you?"

She swallowed when the back of his fingers caressed her cheek. He cupped her chin and tilted her head up. "Yes, I liked it. It was exciting. So what are you proposing?"

"You and me. Together until it isn't fun anymore." His thumb rubbed along her full bottom lip, her body thrown into sensory overload by his soft caress against her hot, moist mouth.

Sienna huffed in a breath, trying to breathe around the sensations he evoked in her. "Sounds really tempting, but I do have something to confess."

"What?" He leaned forward and ran his lips along her jawline.

"My friends challenged me to a dare. Get you in bed and get a souvenir to prove that I actually slept with you."

That confession jerked his lips away from her skin. One corner of his mouth kicked up and a wicked glint appeared in his eyes. "A dare. I like that."

"You would," she said, her voice unnaturally weak.

The glint intensified. His gaze still riveted on her, he rubbed his thumb slowly on her jaw; then he gave her another one of his heart-stopping smiles.

Those cobalt blue eyes riveted to hers not giving her any indication of his next move. So he took her totally by surprise when he framed her face with his hands, tipped her head back and covered her mouth in a full, no-holds-barred kiss.

Shaken and weak, with her heart hammering so hard that she could not catch her breath, Sienna extricated herself from him and backed away.

"After my response to that kiss, it would be lame for me to say you don't affect me. Let's get on this investigation and you cool your jets."

He grinned at that, his eyes dancing with mischief.

"Truce. You go shower and change and we'll go from there. Deal?"

"That's a deal. Although you look good in that uniform, you might want to change. It's a bit conspicuous."

His grin never wavered.

"I've got a duffel with civvies in my truck."

She looked up into his face and couldn't dredge up any animosity. What was wrong with her? Why couldn't she stuff all those feelings in a mental closet? She was normally a levelheaded, practical person, but she knew this for what it was: a losing battle.

ONCE IN the locker room, she indulged herself for one moment by closing her eyes and letting out a long breath.

She'd been right the whole time. A.J. was a dangerous man. What she'd experienced was complex and confusing.

It wasn't like her, she told herself as she took the time to gather her wits. Losing control in the arms of a man felt strange to her. If a man even tried to push her buttons, she put him in his place and received no argument in return. A.J. obviously wasn't just any man.

It was no secret she liked being the button pusher. Rules and regulations dictated her life and she kept that one hard-and-fast rule. Stay in control. But her interaction with A.J. told her he could break that one.

If he got close enough, he could totally break that one.

She'd worked so hard to shape herself into the person she was, laying her life out in very deliberate stages. With inner strength she'd overcome the chaos in her life. With courage and determination she'd beaten it back. She *could* change the blueprint when it was necessary. She wasn't rigid. But nothing, absolutely nothing, jolted the vision.

All that should be on her mind right now was the fact that there was a truckload of guns—including grenade launchers—out on the streets of San Diego and it was her responsibility to keep the city safe. That meant tracking down A.J.'s brother and seeing that justice was served, regardless of the private toll it might take on her or A.J.

She wondered how she was going to keep her professionalism, not to mention her sanity, when it was all over.

RAYMOND MERCHANT, weapons manager for San Diego Naval Base parked his car outside the offices for Taylor Import and Export and wiped his sweaty palms on his jeans. He wouldn't normally come here to talk to Jack Taylor. It only served to make Jack's summons more ominous.

Damn Buckner for panicking and taking the weapons shipment with him, a carefully assembled shipment that had been very difficult to amass right under the Navy's nose.

Getting a job on the huge naval base located in Coronado had been Jack's idea.

But it had been Ray's idea to hire Buckner, who'd been willing to take on the job for money.

When he knocked on the door and was told to come in, Jack was sitting casually behind his desk.

"Ray, make yourself comfortable," Jack said pleasantly as if Ray was there for a social call.

Jack gave him a friendly smile. It made his skin crawl. Ray knew that Jack could not stand incompetence. He knew that because he'd worked for Jack for three years. People who crossed Jack stopped breathing.

Ray sat down. A burly man, who had been sitting in a chair in the corner, stood and strode to Ray's chair, standing at his right elbow. Ray looked up at the hard, dark eyes and quickly turned back around. His heartbeat increased in tempo.

"Corporal Buckner has decided to make this all-important shipment his own."

"How is that?" Ray choked out, wiping the perspiration from his upper lip.

"He's already tried to sell it to one of my rivals."

"How do you know that?"

"I have a man inside." Jack paused and pinned Ray with a cold look. "I'm very displeased."

"Look, Jack, Buckner's spooked. He thinks the

FBI is on to him. He told me he needed to get out of the country. He said he refuses to go to Leavenworth and rot.''

Jack regarded him thoughtfully and made a gesture to the man behind him.

The blow caught Ray on the right temple and he slumped sideways, cupping the side of his face as a trickle of blood oozed slowly down his cheek.

Jack rose from his desk and walked around to lean against its edge. He pulled a pristine handkerchief out of his pocket and handed it to Ray who staunched the blood.

''Ray, I don't give a damn about his motives. I only care about my shipment.''

The icy look in Jack's eyes made Ray's blood freeze. His temple throbbed to the frantic beat of his heart. ''Yes, sir.''

''You find Buckner. Got it? If you don't retrieve my guns, I'll make sure that you never get to spend all that money in your Swiss bank account.''

Ray swallowed.

Jack patted Ray's shoulder, and then he squeezed hard.

''One more thing. Take care of Buckner.'' Jack's words were flat and hollow.

''How do I do that?''

Jack laughed without humor. ''I think you get my drift. Now get out of here.''

Ray didn't argue.

4

WHEN SIENNA EMERGED from the locker room, A.J. was waiting for her. She smelled so good as he fell into step with her.

"Well, you do have good timing. This morning I planned to interrogate the perp we collared on the possession of unlicensed firearms. We found two handguns and a shotgun along with the M-16."

"Why didn't you talk to him right away?" A.J. asked.

"I had a break in another case after I dropped you off on Friday and I've been out straight ever since. I just finished the paperwork for that one late last night."

They made their way swiftly through division headquarters until Sienna stopped at a door. Once inside she indicated the wide glass window. Inside A.J. could see a man sitting at the table. An officer was standing near the door.

"This is Tyrone Knight. I'm going to work on him until I get him to tell me the truth."

"How do you know he's lying?"

"They all lie." She paused and said, "Remember

that I said there were very few coincidences in my job?''

A.J. nodded.

''I think it would be beneficial to show David's picture to Tyrone.''

''You've already condemned my brother? I thought in this country it was innocent until proven guilty?''

''It still is. I just want to rule him out, okay?''

In his heart he was certain his brother couldn't have been associated with anything illegal, not willingly. He reached into his back pocket and pulled out a picture of his brother on the day he'd graduated from college. The year he'd enlisted in the Marine Corps.

Sienna looked at David's picture. ''I can imagine how hard this must be for you. I have a sister and I couldn't imagine how I would handle even the suggestion that she would be involved in something criminal.''

She put her hand on his arm and the warmth of her compassion touched him.

She exited through the door while A.J. waited behind the glass. He wasn't happy about it, but he knew Sienna wouldn't break protocol and allow him into an interrogation room with a suspect, so he hadn't even asked.

But his initial frustration at being stuck behind the two-way glass faded as he watched Sienna work. Her patient, systematic interrogation had a technique all its own. Not only was she thorough, but unyielding, as well.

Tyrone couldn't break her stride or ruffle her cool, professional exterior. She ignored his sarcasm and abusive language and never once raised her voice.

But although she put up a nice solid front for the perp, A.J. wanted to discover what all that sass and vinegar hid. In the short time he'd known her, he'd seen a wide range of emotions from the independent detective. The glimpse of the passion, anger and sympathy was only a sampling of what lay below the surface. Beneath the professionalism, the in-your-face attitude was a richness that he wanted to mine.

"You should be impressed."

A.J. turned toward Captain Sandoval's voice. "I am."

"How about you, Lieutenant? Are you impressive, too?"

"Are you on a fishing expedition to make sure that I can cover Sienna's back? I'm a SEAL. I know all about teamwork."

"Right. Just make sure that you remember that."

"Do you make a habit of attending her interrogations?"

"No. I wanted to check you out. You may be a SEAL, but I don't know you."

A.J. stood silent while Raoul watched Sienna for a moment. She was sitting calm and at ease as Tyrone drummed his fingers on the table.

"How's she doing?"

He felt as if he was going to come out of his skin. "He's still saying that he stole the weapon and ran. But she's holding a trump card."

"What would that be?"

"David Buckner's picture."

"She'll get what she needs from him. The guy doesn't have a chance."

"No doubt." Silence descended as they watched her twist Tyrone into a pretzel.

The moment he dreaded came when Sienna laid the picture of David in front of the perp. The man's face drained of color and he stammered, "N-never seen the guy before."

A.J. closed his eyes against the pain, his brain trying to accept the reality that was staring him in the face.

Sienna sat forward and shoved the picture just a little bit closer. "Take a good look, Tyrone. You wouldn't want to lie to me." Her voice was as cold as steel.

Tyrone closed his eyes, his breathing shallow. "That's the guy."

The man looked as terrified as a trapped rat. Sienna leaned a little bit closer. "Is there anything that you left out of your story?"

"No. I don't have anything else to say."

"I didn't ask you if you had anything else to say. I asked you if you left anything out because there's nothing I hate more than to be jerked around by a punk. We've got you cold on the charges of illegal gun possession. We're running the serial number on that gun, and I'm betting we find that it was stolen from a military base.''

"I told you it was a green truck and it looked like a military truck, didn't I?''

"Yes, you did, so why don't we go over your story again just to make sure that you didn't leave anything out?''

TAKING HER TIME, she'd put Tyrone's statement under a microscope, sucking him dry. She never gave him an inch. When she was satisfied that he'd told her everything he could tell her, she made him write it down. She wasn't convinced it was everything.

She was jazzed as she proceeded to her desk. Yet, she couldn't help feeling sorry for A.J. Tyrone had identified David's picture and her next step was to search David's apartment. The first thing she did when she got to her desk was dial up the assistant district attorney, Jericho St. James.

When he answered the phone, Sienna said, "Jericho, I need a search warrant for the premises of David Buckner…''

"That won't be necessary.'' A.J. said standing next to her desk holding a white paper bag.

"Jericho, never mind. Looks like I'm going to get consent.''

The bleak look in A.J.'s eyes made her crazy. Before she thought about what she was doing, she grabbed his hand.

"I still can't believe that David is voluntarily involved in this, Sienna," he whispered, his voice rough with strain.

"Right now all we have is a lowlife saying yes to David's picture. It's only the beginning of the investigation. I still think Tyrone's holding back on me."

He released her hand and stepped back. "Don't sugarcoat it. I know that David's a suspect."

"A.J., I'll be honest with you. It doesn't look good, that's true, but I never jump to conclusions and you shouldn't, either."

A.J. ran his hand through his hair and her heart squeezed with sympathy for him.

"You'll give me consent to search David's apartment?"

"Yes, but I think you should eat first. I brought you some lunch."

"I've got to find the rest of these guns."

"I agree, but you need nourishment. You didn't even have a doughnut this morning."

"Hmm, looks like I have a funny guy on my hands. Not all cops eat doughnuts. They don't count as nourishment."

"I can see that you keep yourself in great shape."

"Do you think you need to look after me, Camacho?"

"Someone has to. It sounds like you haven't taken a day off in a while."

Sienna shrugged. "I have a job to do and it takes up a lot of my time. Let's check out your brother's apartment."

A.J. opened the bag and the aroma of pastrami and rye hit her hard.

"Okay, we'll take the food with us and eat in the car."

WHEN THEY REACHED the top of the stairs of David's apartment building, his door was ajar. Sienna reached back and pulled out her gun and with the muzzle pointed to the ceiling, motioned him that she was going in.

A.J. followed her, his body on high alert. She darted a quick look around the corner of the doorjamb. With the flat of her hand, she pushed the door open. Leading in with her gun, she went through the ransacked apartment, checking every possible spot a man could hide. A.J. was close behind her.

"There's no one here," A.J. said as he looked around at the destruction. The couch had been ripped up with what looked like a knife. The pictures on the walls had been ripped from their supports, smashed against furniture and hurled across the room.

In David's bedroom, his clothes and uniforms were scattered around the floor, the bed linens dislodged and the mattress ripped to shreds.

"Wonder if they found what they were looking for?" he muttered.

A.J. let his eyes roam around the room, hoping for a clue, anything to tell him where David might have gone. He spied a pair of David's cammie pants lying near the bathroom door. His eyes moved on and spied a yellow piece of paper caught between the bed and the nightstand.

He walked over and reached down.

"A.J., you shouldn't touch anything until the crime scene unit goes over this place."

A.J. ignored her words. He didn't have time to wait around. He picked up the paper and unfolded it. It was a receipt for a U-Haul truck. His stomach sank.

"What is it?" Sienna asked.

He handed the paper to her and Sienna quickly scanned the contents. "Let's head over there and see what we can find out," she said.

A.J. bent down and picked up David's dress uniform jacket, the gold buttons highly polished. A lump formed in his throat. He placed the coat on the mattress and smoothed out the wrinkles.

"I'm sorry, A.J."

"I know." His broad shoulders rose and fell. He turned to pace, but her hand settled on his arm, holding him in place as effectively as an anchor. He looked down into her beautiful face, and the air fisted in his lungs. She looked up at him with dark green eyes full of understanding.

"We'll find him."

A.J. nodded and closed his eyes. But what would they find? Had David gone rogue and decided that the Marine Corps didn't pay enough? Was he disillusioned after his stint in Afghanistan? He thought he knew David, but had his brother drifted away from him during A.J.'s many missions? Did he really know his brother at all?

Sienna called the crime scene unit on her cell phone while A.J. went over to David's smashed and useless computer.

A.J. knelt down and looked at the case. "This might hold useful information."

"I'll have CSI send it over to the cyber forensic guys to see if they can get anything off the hard drive," Sienna said.

He knelt in the mess that had once been his brother's organized apartment and for the first time in his life felt helpless. He didn't like it at all. He was a man of action. He looked down at the picture of his brother posing with A.J. and their mother and father. Sentimental sap had it on his desk near his computer.

The love he had for his brother swelled inside him. "You said you have a sister. Is she older or younger?" A.J. asked.

Sienna smiled at the mention of her sibling. "Younger by seven years."

"You watched out for her?"

"I sure did. You did that for your brother?"

A.J. nodded.

"What is he like?"

He gestured to the picture. "Sentimental, romantic, wants to save the world."

"There's nothing wrong with that."

"What went wrong, then?"

"I don't know."

He turned to her and their eyes met. Slowly they rose. She had the most irresistible mouth, though as he reached for her he knew it was mostly for comfort. Her mouth met his with a tiny little gasp as if an electric shock traveled between them.

His hand went into her hair, cupping her head, feeling his resolve, which he normally held in check, trying to break free.

Heavy footsteps on the stairs forced them apart. She looked up at him as if in shock.

The crime scene unit came through the door, led by Kate.

THEY ENTERED THE U-Haul rental place just after three o'clock.

Sienna walked to the desk and presented the receipt to the clerk. She flashed her badge. "Can you tell me what the license plate is for this truck and the destination?"

"It's our policy not to give information out on our customers. You'll have to get a warrant."

"This is police business and a matter of security."

The clerk gave her a long-suffering look. "Sorry, lady. Get the warrant."

A man entered the office. "Hey, mister, could you give me a hand here? I think the door is stuck on the truck you gave me. If that's the case, I want another one."

The clerk moved from behind the counter and as soon as he was out of sight, A.J. went around to the computer.

"What are you doing?" she hissed.

"We don't have time to get a warrant. It'll take the rest of the day."

"A.J., there are certain procedures that I have to follow."

He grinned. "I don't."

She simmered while he fiddled with the keys.

After a moment he looked up. "Jot this down."

He gave Sienna the license plate number and with a huff, she wrote it down in her notebook.

"The destination is Guaymas-San Carlos," A.J. said.

They exited the rental place and got back in the car. "That wasn't exactly legal."

"He's my brother, I have a right to know where he went. Besides, the guy didn't even know we looked."

"You can't just arbitrarily not follow laws you don't like."

"We're wasting time."

She sat back in her car and put her hands on the wheel, tightening her fingers. "Looks like we're taking a trip to Mexico," she said, picking up her radio and alerting the state police to be on the lookout for the truck. Though she was sure that David would have already left the country by now.

The dispatcher called over the radio to tell them to meet a state trooper at the border crossing. He had information regarding the truck.

It took them twenty minutes to get there. They parked and got out.

"Detective Parker?"

"Yes."

The state trooper approached, flipping through his incident book. "I stopped that truck last night. It had a taillight out."

"Anything suspicious about the truck or driver?"

"No, all routine."

"Did he say where he was headed?" Sienna asked.

"Guaymas-San Carlos. It's a small beach community."

"I know it. It has a seaport."

Back in the car, A.J. looked over at her. "You think he's trucked the guns to this place to ship them out?"

"Possibly. I don't like the trashed apartment. It suggests that someone else is looking for him and they're not very friendly."

"All the more reason to get going. How long?"

"It's a three-hour drive, so buckle up." She picked up her radio again and requested that the Mexico police detain the vehicle and the driver of the U-Haul.

IT WAS much later by the time they pulled into the sleepy little town of Guaymas-San Carlos. Just as eager to get there as he was, Sienna had floored it, using her siren all the way. The radio had crackled around four o'clock that the Mexican police had found the truck and the driver. The address they gave was a hotel on the beach.

A.J. glanced at her as she pulled up to the quaint structure. He was out of the car almost before they stopped.

She was close on his heels as they approached the vehicle. The driver was sitting on the veranda of the hotel, a tan-shirted police officer close by. When A.J. reached them, the driver raised his head.

"That's not my brother." The relief he felt was short-lived. If David wasn't here, where was he?

"What the hell is going on!" the driver demanded.

"SDPD," Sienna said, flashing her badge.

"Not again. Don't you people talk to each other?"

"What do you mean?" Sienna asked.

"I was already bothered by another cop."

"From San Diego?" Sienna asked.

"Yeah. He was looking for someone named Buckner. He was quite insistent. I told him I didn't know the guy."

Sienna pulled out David's picture. "Was this man at the U-Haul rental place when you were picking up your truck?"

The man studied the picture for a moment. "Yeah. He was hovering around the counter when I was signing up for my truck. Asked me if I'd seen his keys."

"He switched the plates," A.J. said quietly.

"Can I go now? I have another delivery to make."

"I just need to take down your information in case I have to contact you."

A.J. walked toward the beach. He stood there watching the water roll to shore. The adrenaline in his system buzzed and he took a deep breath.

Sienna walked up to him and stood close.

"I had half an idea to disarm both you and the cop and get my brother out of there."

Sienna turned toward him. "When did you change your mind?"

"When I realized that it was irrational, stupid and the reaction of a protective brother, not the honorable actions of a Navy SEAL."

Sienna stared out at the ocean. "It's hard to separate the two. If David means as much to you as my sister means to me, I know how you feel."

"Do you find it hard to separate your cop role from your personal life?"

Sienna winced. "Yes, I do. I've missed my dress fitting for my sister's wedding three times. I was so proud and happy when she asked me. I really want to go.''

''Did she understand?''

''No, she was angry. She had every right to be. I told her when she asked me that it might be difficult to get time off.''

''You really should make time, Sienna.''

''I know.'' She was silent for a moment. ''Let's get back to San Diego.''

When they got in the car, she said, ''Although I understand your motives, A.J., I need to know that you're going to keep it together during this investigation. I need to be sure of the guy guarding my back.''

''You can be sure. I love my brother and I want to make sure he's safe. But you have my word. No more foolish thoughts.''

THE TRIP BACK was more leisurely and they'd stopped for a quick dinner in Tijuana.

When they reached the division, A.J. got out of her car, but then leaned back in. The thought of being alone tonight didn't appeal to him. He wanted Sienna wrapped around him. He needed that comfort.

''I want you to follow me back to my apartment.''

She looked up at him, her hair and eyes flaring in the darkness. ''A.J., I don't think…''

''That's right. Don't think,'' he said.

''But…''

"I don't want to be alone. Please come home with me," he pleaded. He wasn't sure what he wanted from this woman, but he was very sure he wanted her close, skin-to-skin close.

"Lead the way," she said softly.

In short order, he was unlocking his apartment door, kicking it shut with his foot.

He shrugged out of his jacket, but Sienna stayed his hand when he went for the buttons on his shirt. "Let's take it slow."

Her hands replaced his, the material pliable against her fingertips. A.J. nuzzled her temple, his gentle breath fanning the soft hairs away from her face.

"Do we have to go this slow?" he rasped softly.

"Impatient? Don't SEALs have to lay in wait for sometimes hours on end?" she whispered, her mouth going to the heated steel muscles she bared. With each button she undid, she kissed the exposed skin, trailing her fingertips along his hard muscles.

He moaned softly on an indrawn breath when her tongue came out and licked his flat nipple. He swallowed as excitement coursed through him. "Do that again," he told her.

She did, this time gently sucking the hard nub.

Breathing hard, his whole body jerked, his head falling back, his eyes closing in sensual rapture as a fiery heat gripped his groin in a tight flaming fist.

His whole body screamed and ached. She looked like a figment of his imagination; the soft illumination in the room seemed to attract to her like a diamond did to light, and even light couldn't resist her. How was he expected to? Just a man, a mortal man. Her eyes were a luminescent green like moss glowing in the moonlight, the dark red strands of her hair softly curving against her cheekbone. His hands itched to be buried in the soft mass.

"Hurry, Sienna, please," he breathed the words and she responded in a husky voice.

"How do you ever get through a mission?"

Heat hit him smack in his stomach, geysered through him turning his blood into volatile liquid.

She drew back, quickly stripping off her clothes. He felt his control slipping its bonds liked a caged tiger escaping a hated prison. He hungered with a voracious appetite for the woman before him.

He wanted her beneath him.

Now.

Her hands swept over the wall of his chest and caressed every inch of his skin. His breathing quickened at the powerful feelings that threatened to overwhelm him.

As his hot mouth slammed into hers, he wanted his kiss to possess her until the need for him was a starving need in her bones. He moved her toward the bedroom and his bed; he could feel her heart hammering against his.

No words were necessary as he backed her purposefully toward the bed. Where she touched he burned; where she didn't touch he ached.

With quick breaths he was able to rein in his passion. Her hands went to his pants and he thrust against her hands as she palmed him through the denim.

"Do you have protection?" she asked.

Everything inside him stilled and he swore and backed up, running his hands through his hair. "No."

She smiled. "I do." She walked over to her purse and as she bent over, he got a tantalizing view of her backside. She turned toward him with foil-wrapped packets in her hand. "I thought SEALs were supposed to be prepared for anything."

"Honey," he said softly, "Those aren't standard issue."

"It's a good thing that I'm always prepared."

"Will you stop waving those around and get back over here?"

"I think you're overdressed. Why don't you take off those pants and show me what is standard issue?"

He laughed and took the two steps to her, pulled her into his arms and took her mouth again.

She gasped and twisted against him at the instantaneous hunger that enveloped her body, at the glorious feel of his hard-muscled frame.

"Why don't you take them off me?"

His thighs were solid and powerful flush up against hers, his chest was unyielding like rock. Sienna could barely draw in breath. There was a very small voice in the back of her head that said, *Be careful.* She mentally slapped it away. This was her daring fling and she was going to take it. Two times with him wasn't a commitment. It wasn't love. It was just sex.

But fantastic, unbelievable sex that overpowered her senses and made her come harder and hotter than she'd ever thought possible.

5

SHE MANEUVERED him toward the bed. When she got there, she pushed on his chest and he tumbled backward. "Are you a pushover, A.J.?"

"For the right woman, I'd do anything." His eyes traveled down her body and she shivered. She'd never done that before. And he had the nerve to lie there with all that glorious muscle primed just for her. His muscles were thick, but cut, delineated in shadow and light from the soft glow of the lamp. His skin was a burnished copper and smooth as silk. In addition to the golden medallion he had around his neck, his dog tags glinted silver in the light, flashing at her.

A warning?

Feeling too much for him wouldn't be smart. He was a SEAL and he wouldn't fit into her orderly world. He'd already proven that by pushing his way into her case and getting the U-Haul information against her wishes.

But she couldn't worry about that now. This was a physical thing. Chemistry.

She placed the packets on the nightstand and leaned

over him, running her hard-peaked breasts against the smooth skin of his chest and abdomen.

His body went rigid and with his head thrown back, he groaned.

Her tongue came out and trailed a path down his ridged stomach to the snap of his pants. "Damn it, Red, you're killing me."

"If I take them off, I'll take them off my way."

"Mmm," he moaned softly when she used her mouth to undo the button and pull down the zipper one slow metal tab at a time. "I like your way."

She gripped the waistband and tugged. A.J. lifted his hips and she discarded his pants in a heap on the floor.

She bent over again and kissed the satin smooth skin at the waistband to his black boxer briefs. "I don't think these are standard navy issue, either."

"I wear white all…" he gasped as her tongue came out and licked his sensitive skin, "…the time," he rasped, his breathing ragged.

His erection strained against the black cotton and Sienna couldn't resist the invitation as she gently bit him through the briefs, then she took the head of his penis in her mouth.

He gasped and his hips came up off the bed. "Ah, Red, that feels good."

She gripped the waistband of his underwear and the tip of his erection peeked out. She suckled him, running her tongue around the velvet skin. With a quick movement, she pulled the underwear down and took all of him into her mouth, sucking hard.

When she released him, she said softly, looking down at him, cupping his hard, hot arousal in her hands, ''This is not standard in any way.''

His body bucked and she found herself grabbed and pulled underneath him.

''You are killing me.''

Her hips undulated in an uncontrollable movement.

''No woman has ever made me laugh and want to be inside her at the same time.''

Her eyes widened at his tortured tone.

He rubbed his shaft against the part of her that ached for him. His voice caught and then he continued, ''How much longer are you going to make me wait?''

She gazed up into his tightly restrained face, her heart skipping a beat at his pleading words.

She touched his face so softly it was almost imperceptible. His body responded as an electric shock coursed along his skin and he closed his eyes. Leaning forward, he gently tasted her lips with his tongue, so sweet.

His eyes dropped down to her breasts, to the hard peaks of her nipples. He could see her creamy skin, her flat stomach, and the dark red thatch of curls at the apex of her thighs, the long sleek legs. His eyes moved up to her face. ''Damn,'' he whispered softly like a man dying and on his last breath. Slowly he reached out with one hand, inexplicably drawn to what enticed him. He'd always been fascinated by the beauty of a woman. But Sienna transcended femininity. The need for her eclipsed everything; every argument he could conceive slipped away like melted honey and the burning hunger once again consumed him.

He gently traced the tip of her nipple. Sienna gasped. She arched her back, a sensuous invitation that he could not ignore.

His hands were all over her body, caressing her, kneading her flesh. He rose to his knees, his eyes flashing like burning sapphire coals.

He moved over her, rubbing himself against her stomach. Sienna felt the glide of his body, the thick shaft of hot skin against her stomach. He slid lower to push against the slick, wet heat of her.

She felt the tension tighten in her body as he massaged the hot core of her. She gasped and moved her hips in an erotic dance against the velvet tip that teased her, sent tingling sensation deep inside her to a place she never knew existed, a place that promised shattering pleasure beyond her imagination.

"Sienna." It came out on a groan as she moved against him.

She never would have guessed it would be like this with him and that thought brought with it uneasiness.

He positioned himself across her body, greedily taking her taunt beckoning nipple in his mouth, sucking it forcefully against the roof of his mouth. Her body bucked.

"Yes, that's it. That's it, sweetheart. Let yourself go."

She loved the sleek moist feel of his muscled skin against her body, beneath her hands, all that powerful energy. He was so male, so desirable. When his mouth took her hard tingling nipple, she convulsed against him; the spiraling energy that had built inside her broke over her in a wave of ecstasy ebbing and flowing, consuming and as vast as the ocean.

Her release pushed him over the edge, too, knowing that he wanted to be inside her, deep inside her, wanted it more than he'd ever wanted anything.

She reared up and grabbed one of the foil packets and ripped it open, sheathing him with one long caress that brought a deep moan to his lips.

She lay back as he moved over her, between her legs. He reached down to guide himself into her, his other hand clenching on the coverlet next to her head. The throbbing need spiraled tighter and tighter, building, escalating higher and higher. He smothered a groan as her wet, hot, satiny flesh yielded to him. His voice was little more than a hoarse growl as he sank into her. Thrusting into her, unable to keep his body from the fulfillment he wanted her to experience with him and the consummation he craved. She jerked against him with a soft cry of pleasure.

His lips closed over hers and she opened her mouth

to his probing, frantic tongue, soothing her hands down the clenched, sweat-soaked muscles of his back.

He thrust frantically into her, never before this out of control. He was and he didn't care. He had to move; motion was imperative, essential. He ached to bring her to release again and join her in the spiraling ecstasy. Her caressing hands moved down his body to his buttocks, bringing him closer, deeper. In response, he drove forward harder, lifting her hips off the bed with the force of his thrusts. He became frantic at the feel of her taking possession of his body, the sweet pressure building in a blinding delirium as he responded to her encouragement, her eagerness to have him all, and the full length of him deep inside her.

The urgency expanded, became all-consuming. He felt as if he had become better somehow. At her harsh cry of satisfaction he anchored himself, grasping her hips tighter as he drove deeply, with long hard frenzied thrusts to the very heart of her need. He didn't slow until he felt the deep spasming of her muscles clenching around him. It was sweet welcome torture beckoning him to join her in her pleasure.

The clasping of her heated sheath and the soft cries deep in her throat sent him careening, spinning. The quick lithe movement of her hips rocking him to the deepest center of his being. He shuddered and cried out his release, a release that was so powerful that he threw his head back so far that the muscles of his throat corded in stark relief.

Sienna relished the sound of his surrender. The response from him was violent, involuntary, as he quivered in his frenzy while driving into her, his passion-stark face tight, his jaw clenching around the rasping groans of sheer undiluted pleasure.

Never had she dreamed that lovemaking could be so all-consuming, so powerful in its release.

Her tongue snaked out and tasted the heated moist skin of his shoulder. He jumped in reaction and moaned softly at the wet heat of her caress.

He tasted salty, male and delicious. The little tremors of her powerful release still vibrated in her inner muscles. He gasped each time she tightened around him, his breathing harsh and breathless.

His mouth was inches away from hers. She could feel the heat; his eyes were an electric blue, and so beautiful they took what little breath she had. Her eyes traveled down the strong column of his neck, her hands came up compelled, seduced into touching him. She traced his collarbone gently. At a rough spot she looked up at him.

"Broke it falling out of a tree." She trailed her finger down to the heavy muscles of his chest where a quarter-size scar felt rough against her sensitive skin. She shivered against him. "Bullet," he said hoarsely.

She leaned into him. Her lips found the scar and

he sucked in his breath sharply. Her mouth moved because she had to taste him; her tongue snaked out and flicked at his hot skin. Thick heated tang of an aroused male burst against her tongue and she made a low, purring sound in the back of her throat.

She ran her finger along a jagged scar on his shoulder.

"Got too close to a grenade."

He moved off her and brought her against his side. With quick movements, he managed to get them both under the covers.

She lay with her head on his shoulder, her hand making lazy circles on the skin of his chest.

"I should go."

"No."

He turned his head, his dark blue eyes slumberous in the dim room. "What are you doing?" he asked.

"Staring at you."

He huffed laughter. Those eyes slid over her like a hot blue flame.

"I really should go," she said, but it was half-hearted. She settled more fully against him. It couldn't hurt to stay for a little while longer.

After a moment, he asked, "What do you hate about police work?"

"You mean besides dragging your sorry ass around with me?"

He smiled; she could feel the rumble of his laughter against her breasts.

"Yeah. Besides dragging me around."

She scrunched up her face. "Paperwork. I hate paperwork."

"I hear you." He nodded.

Raising herself up on her elbow, she asked. "What about you?" Bringing her hand up, she slid it through his damp hair until she reached the nape of his neck. Gently she massaged his muscles.

"I guessed it would be paperwork you hated," he said as his eyes shifted away from her.

It was a classic example of a man not telling the truth. She saw it every day and could pick out a liar in no time. "Don't try to change the subject."

His eyes came back to hers and were suddenly filled with apprehension. "I hate jumping out of airplanes, helicopters. *Any* moving objects."

"Isn't the *A* in SEALs for *Air?* It's supposed to be fun."

"Maybe to thrill seekers and crazy people, but no, not me. I hate the free fall, that limbo before you break the surface of the water. My heart climbs into my throat and it's the closest I come to total panic. And if you repeat this to anyone, I'll deny every word."

Another reason not to become involved with a man who put himself in dangerous situations every day. The thought of him free-falling out of a helicopter made her blood run cold. "Are you afraid to die, A.J.?"

"SEALS are invincible." He smiled, but sobered when she didn't smile back. "No. I'm not afraid to die, Sienna. Dying is easy. It's the living that's hard."

"You have a bullet wound, so you've not only been shot at, but have been wounded."

"Oh, yeah. Been shot at, been shot. Didn't like it. Wouldn't recommend it. How about you?"

"When I was on foot patrol, I chased down a burglary suspect. I didn't know he had a gun. When he turned it on me and fired, I really wasn't thinking at all. I guess it made me mad. I was the police. Who did this little punk think he was? I rammed right into him. Took him down and cuffed him. I don't know who was more surprised, him or me."

"You seem young to be a detective."

"In years or experience?" she asked.

"Definitely in years."

She shrugged. "I caught a lucky break."

"I don't believe in luck. I think you make your own luck."

"That so?"

"Sure. Some people acquire the skill and they hone it over years, others have an innate ability. What was your lucky break?"

"I was working vice and had been on the force for four years. I'm strolling around on these three-inch heels in my skimpy hooker outfit night after night. It was so boring. But even though I'm bored, I keep my eyes open. After working that street for a week, I have the patterns down. Who goes where, who does what, you know.

"About the second day, I notice there seems to be a lot of activity at this one garage."

"What's so strange about cars going in and out of a garage?"

"Nothing. But this is eleven and twelve at night."

"Chop shop?"

"That's what I think. So I keep watching this place all the while I'm doing my hooker bit. Finally, I have to go check the place out and I mention to my partner what I think is going on. After our shift, we go over and take a look. I can see that there's a transaction going on inside and it has nothing to do with cars being cut up for parts."

"Drugs?"

"Yes, a huge operation. My partner and I nabbed three of the city's biggest. We confiscated seventy-five kilos of heroine. I got a promotion out of it. I was in the right place at the right time."

"Sounds to me like you used observation and brains to make the bust."

"Maybe. All I know is that I felt as if I'd really done something important. Not that patrolling the streets and keeping order isn't important, but getting all those drugs off the street and away from potential victims was satisfying."

For a moment he stared into her eyes, then he lifted

his head and chest off the mattress and brushed a light kiss against her lips. Then he groaned.

"Your enthusiasm is contagious," he whispered against her mouth.

He covered her mouth in a hot starving kiss, and his hands delved into her hair, kneading her scalp.

Weakness flooded through Sienna. He pressed her back into the mattress. Then his hot, wet mouth was on her skin and it wasn't enough. Her breasts ached with need. As she arched against him, his mouth took her nipple.

It was like being touched by a high-voltage wire, and Sienna made a low sound, succumbing to the urgency clamoring in her. His mouth moved to her other breast. A frenzied weakness pumped through her when she felt him harden against her thigh. Another low sound was driven from her as A.J. nipped her ever so slightly, deliciously. Increasing the pressure of his mouth as if some grinding need had broken loose, Sienna felt as if she were drowning in the heat, in the sensations, in the drugging pleasure he created in her.

Sienna held on to him, her fingers kneading the thick muscles of his back. She gave herself—everything, all that she was and felt as if she'd been freed from a prison of isolation.

She reached down, molding her hand over the length of his arousal. A.J. jerked against her, his fingers snagging in her hair. The way he pressed himself against her made Sienna sob his name.

A.J. grabbed her hands. "Wait. Protection."

She rolled and pushed A.J. onto his back. Grabbing another foil pouch, she opened the packet and sheathed him.

A.J. shuddered, his arms coming up around her. Roughly grasping the back of her head, he angled her face and took her mouth in another wild, plundering kiss. Cupping her buttocks, he twisted his pelvis against her. Lifting her hips to seek relief from the heavy ache inside him, he began thrusting against her, his mouth hungry and wild. With a cry, Sienna clutched at his broad shoulders. He grabbed her around the waist, flipping her onto her knees, dragging her back against his chest and rock-hard thighs. His hand splayed against her flat stomach, he leaned into her seeking her feminine core. She couldn't stand the swelling, throbbing heaviness in her. She couldn't stand the almost unbearable pleasure of the feel of his hot skin against hers. She couldn't stand the torment of waiting anymore. "A.J.," she ordered. "Please."

"Red, you are so beautiful," he said raggedly, his chest expanding on a groan.

"Inside me," she demanded. "Now, A.J."

A violent tremor coursed through him and he buried his face in her curls, his whole body rigid with a shattering tension. The hand against her stomach slipped down, cupping her heat, his fingers sliding over her as he began stroking her.

With a slow, hot glide he entered her. Buried deep inside her, he rocked against her, and Sienna lost her tenuous hold on reality.

A.J.'s hands came to her hips, holding her as he moved fiercely against her. She called out in a wild voice as she splintered a second time, arching against the length of A.J.'s powerful body.

With a strangled groan, he convulsed against her, clutching at her hips. His body jackknifed as he pumped until his body went rigid and he achieved his release.

They collapsed into each other's arms. A.J. pulled the covers over them once more. Their breathing slowed and a languorous feeling came over her. She curled against him and it wasn't long before she drifted off.

She woke with a start. Glancing at the bedside clock she saw it was two o'clock Tuesday morning.

She got up and went to the bathroom. When she was finished, she'd had every intention of getting back into bed with him. She liked the idea of having breakfast with him in the morning. But as she was making her way around the bed, the open closet door caught her eye. The uniform that hung there made her heart skip a beat.

Drawn to the navy whites, she fingered the material

and that edginess inside her returned. He'd done what she feared he would. Distracted her from her routine and the responsibility of her job. There was so much work on her desk. Other cases she'd neglected since she'd met tempting A.J.

Living in the San Diego area made it almost impossible not to be exposed to the military, especially the navy. With Coronado just across the bridge, the nightclubs were filled with navy personnel. Sienna wasn't immune to the spit and polish of that type of man—dedicated, resourceful and loyal.

But Special Forces were a different type all together. And SEALs were in a class by themselves.

Best leave this as a surface thing and not spend the night in his arms. A whisper of panic shivered through her. There was something very intimate about waking up together, eating together.

She looked over at A.J. and felt a pang in her chest. It would be smart to leave now.

She let go of the uniform, made her way over to her clothes, and dressed quickly. She paused and turned, taking one more look at him. With a hunger that was new to her, she slipped out the door.

6

_____

KATE QUINN WAS at her desk, her head bent over a file folder.

"Hi, Kate," Sienna said, setting down a grande mocha on her desk.

"Yum, thanks," Kate said, pushing her tortoise-shell reading glasses into her thick blond hair. She reached for the cup and took a sip of the coffee. She studied her friend. "I'm no trendsetter, but isn't it a fashion gaffe to wear the same clothes twice?"

Sienna smiled and sat down in one of the chairs in front of her cluttered desk.

She sipped from her own chai tea. "I was with A.J. After I left his place, I couldn't sleep, so I came here."

Kate snorted and said, "Right. Our home away from home." She took another sip and savored the taste. "So how goes it with the SEAL? Any trouble?"

"Yes, in that he's still around. And no, in that he's a really interesting guy."

"Did you sleep with him yet?"

"Yes, I slept with him twice."

"What's wrong?" Kate studied Sienna's face. "You're not falling for this guy, are you?"

"Maybe a little. That's really why I left. I was feeling…I don't know…proprietary. He's not mine. I told you both that A.J. and I weren't compatible. There's no future relationship for us."

"But…?"

"I can't deny that he makes me feel alive. I've never felt this way about a man, Kate. We didn't even make it out of the building on Friday night."

"What? Details!"

"We had the most mind-blowing sex in the elevator. That was before he pulled strings with his senator father and got himself assigned to work this stolen military weapons case with me. His brother is involved and it really looks like Buckner stole military weapons and is trying to sell them. I think he's got a badass on his tail."

"Right, the weapon that was taken off—" she consulted her notes "—Tyrone Knight. You asked me to check with the FBI on the serial number."

Setting her tea aside, Sienna rested her elbows amid a maze of file folders and printouts. "That's why I'm here. Have they called you back yet?"

Kate bent down and opened the desk file drawer and searched through it. She pulled out a manila file and glanced at it. "They haven't. That's strange because I got the information on the other firearms you confiscated from his car, but not on the military weapon.'' Kate consulted her notes. ''The shotgun was purchased legally, but the two handguns were stolen from a shipment in Colorado.''

''They were? Hmmm, seems like Tyrone and I need to have another little chat.''

Sienna took the file out of Kate's hands and picked up the phone. She dialed the FBI and waited while it rang. When the person picked up the line, Sienna stated who she was and what she needed.

The receptionist transferred her to the lab and they put her on hold. She glanced at Kate and leaned back against the chair, the fatigue dragging at her.

Kate tilted her head and gave her a scolding look. ''I'm telling this to you as a friend, Sienna. Get more sleep. It's clinically proven that sleep deprivation will take years off your life.''

''Spoken like a true scientist.'' Sienna switched her attention back to the phone as the lab attendant came back on the line.

''Detective Parker, we're very sorry, but somehow we overlooked that serial number when we were processing Ms. Quinn's request. We'll try to get to it as soon as possible,'' he said without an ounce of apology in his voice. If anything, he sounded annoyed and distracted.

''Make it a priority. I needed that information yesterday,'' she ordered.

''We'll do the best we can,'' he promised.

Sienna ended the call. "Great. Lab mix-up. Would you call me the minute you get the report?"

"I will. Keep me updated on your progress."

"With the case?"

Kate rolled her eyes. "No. With the SEAL."

Sienna rose, giving Kate a grin in acknowledgement. "I've got to go. Gotta check in with the cyber geeks and see what progress they've made on Buckner's smashed computer, and check on a list of gunrunners active in the San Diego area, which I requested this morning."

"I'll see you later. Hopefully, I'll be having some hot sex of my own soon," Kate said, giving Sienna a cheeky smile.

"You bet, girlfriend. We'll make sure that Jericho St. James doesn't overlook you." With a wave Sienna slipped out of Kate's office.

A.J. HAD BEEN cooling his heels in Sienna's office for an hour. He was impatient to find out why she'd left him without even a note. He also had to admit to himself that he was miffed about it.

To take his mind off the reason he was miffed, he flipped through some of the files on her desk. The reports were filled with that strange cop jargon, a language that was both succinct and elaborate. Suspects were in possession of controlled substances, committing a B and E and aggravated assault.

Although Sienna had told him she hated paperwork, she wrote a damn good report. Rules-and-Regulations Parker, he thought and closed the file. Maybe most of his anger came from the fact that he wasn't prepared to accept that there was a lot more to her than the straight-arrow cop.

He'd seen her track down leads like a bloodhound, her eyes alive with determination. He'd felt her electric response, a spontaneous and burning embrace. Most importantly he couldn't ignore her deep compassion.

There had been plenty to take in, but he knew there was more beneath that tough-cop act.

David was his priority, had to be. Yet Sienna was like a loaded gun with a hair trigger—dangerous.

It made him angry. It made him edgy. And when she swept into the room, a printout under her arm, it made him snarl.

"I've been waiting for an hour. Where have you been?"

She gave him a cool look as he took in her disheveled clothes, the dark circles under her eyes.

"You've been here all night?" he said.

"I couldn't sleep."

"So, you left without telling me or leaving me a note."

"I didn't want to wake you. Besides, I don't have the luxury of working one case like TV cops. I have to go to court the day after tomorrow and I needed to prepare."

"I think you find it easier to duck out instead of dealing with your feelings."

She looked at him as if he'd struck her. He didn't know he was going to say that. The deep gut feeling that something was churning below the surface of this woman set off unknown instincts he didn't know he possessed.

He didn't want to leave this as sex and it cut him deep inside to think that it was easy for her to do so. *Easy* wasn't the right word. He could see that now as she met his gaze. There was a wealth of emotion in her eyes, confusion, apology and fear. There was nothing simple about this woman.

"A.J....." she began. She broke off, swearing when her phone rang.

"Parker." She slipped into her chair as she spoke, her hand already reaching for a pencil. "Yeah. Yeah, I got it." She broke the connection and rose from her desk, all business.

"The list and this conversation are going to have to wait."

He let out a deep breath and rubbed the back of his neck where most of his tension had lodged. She was tired, he realized, tired and strung out. A woman who did her job with precision and intelligence... The personal stuff was going to have to wait. "Why?"

"They found the military truck."

A.J.'S STOMACH SANK when he saw the vehicle parked behind one of David's favorite hangouts, a bar by the name of Mahoney's. The passenger side window was smashed in and glass lay on the seat and on the pavement.

"The truck is empty," a uniformed officer said. "Crime scene is on the way."

Kate pulled up just as the words left the officer's lips. She got out of her car and walked toward Sienna.

"Looks like we're seeing each other sooner than we thought," Kate said.

"Never a dull moment. Look, when you dust for prints, if you get anything, let me know. Send it right off to the FBI for identification."

"Will do." Kate smiled at Sienna and nodded toward A.J. "Lieutenant Camacho."

A.J. nodded back.

Back in the car, Sienna picked up the radio and told the dispatcher she was heading over to the warehouse district. A.J. recognized the address. It was the one Tyrone had given Sienna over and over during his interrogation.

"Why are we going there?" A.J. asked.

"I want to comb the area again for any possible witnesses. I did an initial canvass and couldn't find anyone who saw anything. But after I talked to Kate this morning and found out that Tyrone had two illegal handguns from a stolen Colorado shipment, I'm questioning his story."

It was noon when she pulled up to the place where

they had found David's car. Sienna got out and looked around. She turned her head at the sound of construction and A.J. followed her as she headed in that direction.

A crew was working on repairing one of the warehouse roofs.

Sienna approached one man who directed her to the foreman. When they reached the guy, he was talking to one of the roofers.

"Excuse me," Sienna said, flashing her badge. "Were you here at all on Thursday?"

"Sure was. This about the open gun transaction?"

"You saw a gun buy?"

"I called the police on Friday, but you people kept me on hold too long. I hung up. I meant to call you back, but have been busy trying to get these shingles in time to do this roof."

"Could I get your name for the record?" she asked.

"Mike Calzone."

Sienna jotted it down. "Could you describe what you saw?" Sienna prompted.

"Sure. I'm on the roof measuring for product when I happen to glance toward the back parking lot. A military truck and a sedan drive in. This warehouse is being renovated, so it's pretty deserted around here.

"One guy gets out of the truck and the other guy gets out of the sedan. Then a red convertible pulls up. Another guy gets out. They talk for a while. The driver of the truck and the driver of the sedan get into the sedan and leave.''

"Then what?''

"The convertible driver waits by the truck until another guy drives up in a black Mercedes. He comes over. The convertible driver pulls a weapon out from the back of the truck and hands it to the guy.''

"M-16?''

"Yes. I'm sure of it. I used to be in the army, now I'm retired. A siren sounded, I can see it's an emergency vehicle a couple of blocks away. The guy with the automatic weapon must have thought it was the cops. So he bolts, gets into his car and speeds away.''

"What did the truck driver do?''

"He yells at the guy, but it doesn't do any good. Finally he gets in the truck and drives off.''

She pulled out David's picture and handed it to Mike. "Is this the man who was driving the convertible and then drove away in the truck?''

Mike studied the picture for a few minutes. "It was from a ways away, but that looks like the guy.''

"Sir, thank you for your help.'' She handed him her card. "Could you please call me if you remember anything else?''

"Sure will. You guys shouldn't put someone on hold for so long.''

"I'll pass that along.''

When they were out of earshot, Sienna turned to

A.J. "Looks like David was involved. Tyrone was apprehended in a black Mercedes."

"This is hard for me to accept." But faced with irrefutable evidence that a witness placed David at the scene with Tyrone Knight engaging in an illegal gun transaction, A.J. could only feel sick in the pit of his stomach.

"It would be hard for anyone who loves a brother to accept. You're human."

Back at the car, A.J. asked, "What now?"

"We're going to take another swing at Tyrone, but first I need to generate another list."

"What list?"

"Early this morning I ran a list of possible gun-runners, thinking we might be able to narrow it down to perhaps one or two who would be involved in stolen military shipments, but the list was too long."

"You know a way to narrow it down?"

"Yes, I do." She got into the driver's seat and turned to him as he settled into the passenger one. "I told you they always lie."

AT HER DESK the keys of the computer felt cool to her touch as she accessed the search parameters on the database she needed and typed in the pertinent details. A.J. was sitting in a chair to the right of her watching her.

"What are you doing?"

"I'm cross-referencing Tyrone with known gun-runners to see if there's any connection."

"You sound confident you're going to find one."

"I am confident. I think Tyrone works for one of them. Tyrone was a buyer for someone."

"Which means that David was the seller."

"Right."

A single sheet of paper spit out of her printer and Sienna picked it up.

She smiled like a cat who had just discovered the canary cage open. "Bingo."

She still had that smile on her face when she walked into the interrogation room the second time. This time A.J. went in with her.

Tyrone reacted to that smile just the way she hoped. His eyes took on a wary look. He studied A.J. the way one warrior studies another.

"I've told you everything I know. Do we have to go over this again?"

Sienna placed a file on the table and took her time in sitting down and getting comfortable. "Oh, Tyrone, I just wanted you to know that I traced the handguns in your car."

She waited a beat for that information to settle in.

He swallowed hard and shifted his gaze away from her knowing eyes.

"Seems they were stolen, too."

"I bought those—"

"Don't bother denying it. Oh, by the way. This is

David Buckner's brother. He's a Navy SEAL and I heard they know how to bruise a man without leaving a mark.''

''Why you telling me that?''

''You're a smart guy, Tyrone. Although, your choice of employer does leave something to be desired.''

Sienna picked up the result of her search and slid the paper over to him.

''What's this?'' Tyrone said, picking up the paper as if it were a live snake.

''I cross-referenced your name with all known gunrunners in our handy dandy database, and guess who bailed you out of jail?''

''Estaban Rojas,'' Tyrone said, closing his eyes. ''You're looking for David Buckner?''

''Him and the stolen military weapons. A little cooperation would go a long way.''

''No lady, you've got that part wrong. It'd be a short trip six feet under.''

A.J. shifted and Tyrone fidgeted in his chair.

Sienna inclined her head. ''I could offer you police protection, as much as that sticks in my craw.''

''Right.'' Tyrone snorted. ''Cops with me 24/7. Are you crazy? No, thank you. I've had enough of your kind of hospitality.''

''That's too bad. My heart is breaking for you.'' She used her disinterest as another tool, slowing down the pace of the interview until Tyrone was squirming in his chair. "It's really simple, Ty. If you don't tell me what you know, you're on your own."

"I'll take my chances."

"That's fine. You may make bail on the gun charges—probably deal them down so you may not do any time. But word has a way of spreading. It's a crying shame the way criminals are such gossips." She let that thought simmer in his brain. "Don't you think that Rojas knows you've been scooped up? He's no dummy. If I have information that only you could tell me, well, you do the math."

"I didn't tell you anything."

"Not a math genius, I see. One way or another, I'm going to get Rojas and when I do, I'll let you go. What do you think old Estaban is going to think?" Casually she opened a file and produced a list. "He might wonder if I got this list as a result of you telling us about that stolen Colorado shipment."

"I didn't give you anything." Sweat popped out on Tyrone's forehead as he stared at the list.

"That's the funny thing about police officers. We can stretch the truth. It's like rubber. You know, Ty," she added leaning toward him, "some people add two and two and get five. Happens all the time."

"That ain't legal." He moistened his lips. "It's blackmail."

"We could get along just fine, Ty." She nudged the list toward him. "If you could find it in your heart to stop lying as easily as you take breath, maybe I'd carc if you ended up feet first at the morgue.'' She smiled. ''If we were best buddies, I'd make sure my friends were taken care of maybe with a new identity, a new life.''

Something flickered in his eyes. She knew it was doubt. ''You talking witness protection program?''

''Now you're doing the math. Only problem is that a big favor like that needs something strong to grease the wheels.'' When he hesitated, she sighed. ''You better choose sides, pal. Gunrunners do not have a sense of humor.''

The fear was back in his eyes. ''I get immunity. And you drop the gun charges.''

''Ty, Ty...'' Sienna shook her head. ''You scratch my back and I'll scratch yours. You give me Rojas. I give you something back. It's how the game is played.''

He licked his lips again, ''I'll give you Rojas.''

''Keep talking.''

''Buckner drives for Taylor.''

''Jack Taylor.''

''Right. Buckner's worried that the FBI is on to him, paranoid about being under suspicion so he hijacked Jack's cargo for some quick cash to get out of the country.''

''So Rojas was purchasing Taylor's cargo?''

''Yeah. Buckner could have asked for what he wanted and Rojas would have given in.''

"Why?"

"Rojas hates Taylor and would love to take something away from him and rub his nose in it."

"Now let's talk about the Colorado shipment."

7

It was late evening when they parked out in front of Rojas's office and went up to the front door. Even with Tyrone's statement, it had taken her the rest of the day to obtain a search warrant for the stolen weapons. Sienna knocked, but after ten minutes no one came.

"Where is that little weasel?" Sienna said under her breath. She turned to A.J. "I'm going to check out back. Stay here."

"But…"

"No buts. You stay put, no matter what. I'm just going to check it out."

"Sienna…"

"A.J., just do what I say."

A.J. sighed and reluctantly nodded, turning back to the front door as Sienna's form slipped around the office building and disappeared.

Five minutes passed and no one came to the door. A.J. was getting restless when all of a sudden he heard the unmistakable sound of automatic gunfire.

He ran to the car and grabbed up the shotgun there and headed around the building at a run. When he reached the back, he saw Sienna crouched down behind a Dumpster, close to a dark sedan from which three men were firing at her. They hadn't seen him, so he went down onto his belly, crawling until he skirted the Dumpster. He used a Mack truck to hide behind.

Sienna peeked around the Dumpster and returned fire, giving A.J. the opportunity to crouch and stalk quietly along the side of the sedan.

"Hold your fire!" he yelled as he popped up right at the bumper and all three men stopped shooting at Sienna. "Drop your weapons!"

They complied. As soon as the order was given Sienna came out from behind the Dumpster, pulling a set of handcuffs from her belt.

"Facedown," she ordered. But out of the corner of A.J.'s eye he saw a long black muzzle and a finger slip down to its trigger. He screamed Sienna's name and she jerked upright, her guard dropped. Without hesitation, without thinking about how easy it would be for the man to turn his weapon on him, A.J. sprang headlong at the hidden shooter.

In the instant that A.J. collided with him, a rapid succession of explosions nearly deafened him. He went down to his knees, stunned. He heard a scuffling, but it was only a faint sound through the ringing in his ears. A little dazed, he rolled to avoid the butt end of the automatic weapon. With a scissoring motion of his legs, he tripped up his assailant and knocked the guy to the pavement. With a quick succession of punches, the man was unconscious.

After A.J.'s lifesaving shout and flying leap into the hidden man with the gun, Sienna had her hands full taking down the first two men who had launched themselves at her. She had dispensed with them just as the third dived for one of the dropped weapons and brought it up.

But Sienna was already moving, executing a kick that sent the gun spinning out of the man's hands. Her second kick sent him flying into the big black sedan, his head slamming against the passenger's side window. The window broke, sending glass flying.

"I'll kill you, you bitch."

He picked up a metal tube that had been discarded on the ground and hit her a glancing blow to the shoulder. She stumbled, slipped on some oil and went down. Glass bit into her forearm, but the pain was there and gone in a white-hot burst as adrenaline swept it away.

She scrambled to her feet and went into a fighter's crouch. She ducked his wild swing, coming up and punching him hard in the soft flesh of his underarm. The man gasped in pain and tried to grab her around the neck. Sienna danced away and delivered a roundhouse kick that sent her attacker to his knees.

It wasn't until after she'd cuffed him and read him

his rights that she saw that A.J. was tying up the gunman he'd dealt with.

Her eyes met his and something fizzled along her nerve endings, the same kind of feeling she'd felt when Lana had pushed her out from under that beam.

Without breaking eye contact, she pulled out her cell phone and called the division asking for backup, stating she'd just walked into a major arms deal.

She couldn't get around the fact that he'd saved her life. She'd missed that fourth man. It would have been a costly mistake if A.J. hadn't been there to back her up.

Sienna didn't know how long she stood there staring at him, meeting those intense blue eyes, expressive and gorgeous. Somehow that didn't seem as terrifying as it should have been.

A.J. gave her a slight smile and Sienna could barely contain the raw and turbulent feelings that rushed through her.

She broke her gaze when she heard the sirens wailing as they got closer and closer. The intimacy didn't fade although she was across the parking lot from him. It was still there, swirling around her, making her feel things that she'd never thought she'd ever feel.

The cold hard truth hit her. She'd never wanted to rely on anyone before, but in the short time that she'd known A.J., she had this sudden urge to lean. It was too dangerous to even think about it. Too dangerous to contemplate what would happen if she let herself feel too much, want too much.

The patrol cops took the men away as Sienna gave her statement.

WITH THE SURGE of adrenaline still ping-ponging around in his body, A.J. was in his element. Search and destroy was something he excelled in. Yet, he'd been a bit slow off the mark, another reminder that the grenade had done more damage than was possible to heal.

When he'd taken down the hidden man, he had to check his fury. A.J. knew many ways to kill a man and he would have used deadly force if he thought there had been any more of a threat from the downed man. There was no way that anything would happen to Sienna, not on his watch.

She was calm and professional as she gave her account to the patrol officers and relinquished the suspects to them.

He relived that moment when her eyes had met his. She had been shaken and he knew why. He suspected that Sienna didn't make many mistakes and considered it a weakness to do so.

He watched her from a short distance talking to Captain Sandoval who had showed up on the scene about ten minutes ago.

A.J. came up to her, his emotions shut down in order to keep himself from acting unprofessionally by taking her into his arms.

"I want a full inventory of those weapons and a

list of serial numbers on my desk in an hour," she blurted.

"I think under the circumstances, you ought to go home," A.J. said.

"No. These weapons could be the ones. I need to interrogate Rojas."

"Sienna. You're bleeding and exhausted. You need to rest."

"No," she shook her head emphatically, the cop to the core, not willing to leave a job undone.

"The guns and Rojas aren't going anywhere."

"But your brother...?" she persisted.

He admired her tenacity and he was worried sick about his brother, but in this case, further interrogation of Rojas wouldn't get them anything.

"My brother's not here. I searched the building, while you were talking to the uniforms. After Rojas tried to shoot you and I took him down, I asked him where David was."

"Maybe you didn't ask him the right question."

"I was very persuasive," he said, arching his brow, his mouth kicking up into a grim smile. "Believe me, if he knew where David was, he would have said so."

She studied his face and then said wearily. "Do I even have to mention that using non-police methods can cause problems with a case, like maybe he could use a loophole to get out of prosecution?"

"I didn't leave any bruises," he said.

She rolled her eyes and sighed. Her shoulders slumped, "You think this is a dead end?"

"I think that it can wait until tomorrow."

"Not if we can get another lead."

"Parker, go home," Raoul said firmly. "That's an order." He put a hand on her arm. "Two big busts in one week are enough for any cop. Even you."

A.J. nodded to the captain in acknowledgement. At least she couldn't argue with her boss.

"Captain, you told me to get those guns off the street. That's what I'm doing."

"You can't track anything if you drop from exhaustion," A.J. said quietly.

Sienna's mouth thinned. "Looks like I'm outgunned and outranked. Hobart," she called to one of the uniforms. "Get one of these guns to Kate Quinn in the lab. Have her call me at home."

The uniform nodded his head. A.J. took the opportunity to usher Sienna toward his car, waiting for the explosion, waiting for her to tell him that he'd disobeyed her order to stay put.

He wondered how he was going to get out of this one. He'd rather make love to her instead of fighting with her.

All the way to her apartment, he pondered her hold over him. Every single moment he spent with her still didn't seem enough. They'd been together almost twenty-four hours and he wanted more.

He wanted ties with her.

He shocked himself when he realized that he wanted commitment.

He didn't want nonobligatory sex with a woman who didn't need him for anything other than to reciprocate the nonobligatory part. He wanted honesty and intricacy. He was moving into a complicated zone, but he couldn't seem to care. After realizing how close she had come to a fatal shooting, he understood how much he wanted to explore every multifaceted inch of her.

Then he thought about how demanding his job was and how special a person had to be to put up with a SEAL's schedule. It was foolish to let his emotions take hold of him, but where Sienna was concerned, he found it hard to care.

She was definitely having second thoughts about him. Why else would she have left last night?

He was moving into hazardous territory filled with land mines dangerous to the heart. He had vowed from the beginning he would steer clear of any woman who needed more from a man than sex. But he couldn't seem to help himself.

He felt much more for Sienna than he wanted to. He'd been moved by her simple offer of compassion, her interest in his training and the importance of the SEALs to him. Sharing this deep stuff with her had changed his perception of being part of a relationship. The special give and take that a man and woman experienced while moving closer to something... permanent.

The navy had been his life for a long time. The SEAL team he commanded was his family and it had been enough. Enough until the red-haired vixen with the tight green dress had asked him for a dance.

He came around the car to help her out and she looked up at him with a whimsical look on her face that said she wasn't an invalid. He studied her up-turned face, trying to gauge her state of mind, but she was like a closed book, giving nothing away. He bet she was one hell of a poker player.

He followed her to the elevator, to her door and then inside her apartment.

When he closed the door, she said very quietly, "You were supposed to stay put."

"I know, but—"

She put her fingers over his lips to silence him. She looked up at him, her eyes wide, her fingers soft against his mouth.

"You never do anything you're told. I wonder how you ever live a military life."

"If you're going to read me the riot act..." he said around her fingers.

"Thank you," she whispered, cutting him off, "for saving my life."

He looked down at her, surprised that she acknowledged the fact.

Damn, she was beautiful, standing in the glow of

the moon cast through her large windows. Like a sweet angel come to earth minus only the halo and wings. Something shifted inside him as he stared down at her, and he suddenly wanted to be the kind of man she needed.

He gathered her up and pulled her tightly against him, realizing that he could have lost her tonight. It shook him how much that thought made his heart skip a beat with fear and something else.

"It was my pleasure, Red," he whispered hoarsely against her hair. He smoothed her locks back with his thumb, then brushed his mouth against her temple. She reached up and cupped his jaw, her fingers gentle and warm against his skin.

That innocent caress took the breath right out of him, and he turned his face against hers. She froze for just a moment, as everything seemed to spin down to utter calm and stillness, then she sucked in a sharp breath when he lifted her face. Neither of them even gasped as he covered her mouth in a searing kiss.

Her mouth was hot as sin; a low, rough sound escaped his lips. No woman in his past had ever generated this kind of heat, this urgent need to sink into her in every way he could. The warm, lush feel of her was beyond his imagination as he savored the forbidden taste of her. He soaked up the sensations of the silk of her hair against the rough tips of his fingers, the softness of her breasts against his chest.

He ran his hands down her arms and his palm came

in contact with something wet and sticky. He broke the kiss and flipped on the hall light.

"You're bleeding," he said, all the desire draining out of him at the sight of the blood on her blouse.

"And it stings like hell, I don't mind saying."

He lifted her chin to get a better look at her eyes. Dark green, weary pools, as if she fought a draining internal battle. He thought she might be on the last remainder of her energy. The protective feeling that descended over him was sudden, he couldn't deny that he wanted to take care of her.

Gently, he unbuttoned the cuff and peeled the torn, grimy silk away from the skin of her forearm. With as much gentleness as his big hands could muster, he inspected the injury in the bright light of the hall. There was a small cut near her elbow. It didn't look deep enough to require a hospital or stitches, but it was slowly oozing blood with dirt and shards of glass clinging in the sticky mess.

When he moved her arm to check for any other sign of injury, she clutched at her shoulder with a soft cry.

"I'm sorry," he whispered, stroking her dirt-streaked face.

She managed a smile for him to lessen his guilt. "It's okay. It really doesn't hurt that bad."

"Right," A.J. said softly. "This needs cleaning up and a bandage."

"I can do it myself," Sienna bristled.

"Yeah, well, you aren't going to."

"I don't need to be coddled."

"Maybe not," A.J. said, slipping his arm around her shoulder. "But I need to coddle you."

He led her to the bathroom and reached for the button of her shirt.

"I can do it," she said in an irritated voice.

He let her.

He clenched his jaw as she undid the buttons and struggled out of the shirt, wincing a little. This was just about him helping her to clean her wound, not about how the sight of her stirred him. He wanted to take care of her, help her out. But as the shirt slid down her shoulders, revealing a see-through white, gauzy bra, he could see her nipples were puckered and a succulent pink.

He was hard-pressed not to remember how he had rolled those nipples between his fingers, sucked on them until she'd cried out his name. His breath came a little harder, his jeans got a little tighter as his gaze followed the swell of her breast above the sexy bra.

Then she raised her arm to push at her hair and the ugly cut on her forearm came into view, the sight of it sending guilt to tighten his chest. Jeez, could he stop thinking about her in a sexual way for five minutes?

"Have a seat," he ordered gruffly.

He saw how she tried not to react when he applied the antiseptic, but she couldn't help it as she made a small noise. "Can we talk about the real reason you left my apartment last night?"

She looked up at him, startled by his question. "I told you that I couldn't sleep, so I went into work."

"That's bull and you know it. How long have you been hiding behind your job when the emotional stuff starts getting too much for you to handle?"

"You just don't like being second fiddle to my job," she snapped.

"Well, now that you mention it, no, I don't like it."

"I'm trying to find your brother and clear this case. Why do we have to get bogged down with hurt feelings?"

"Sienna…"

"It was you who said it was just fun."

"Are you going to tell me that you don't feel it?"

"Feel what?"

"That buzz along the skin, the bond that's forming."

"It's natural to form a bond. We have a common goal."

"No," he growled. "I'm talking about this. When I touch you, I want to be closer, know all your secrets."

She sighed and rested against him. "Okay, you win. I feel it. Are you happy now?"

"That's good to hear." He leaned in close, his

warm breath sending goose bumps all over her body. "I was afraid you didn't care."

She reached out her uninjured arm and cupped his cheek in her hand. "No. Don't think that. I just need some time to assimilate this. I thought we'd be a one-night stand and it's now much more than that."

He smiled, clasping her around the waist. He helped her rise.

"I feel caught off guard, too. You're not what I expected."

He moved a little away from her, but didn't let go of her waist. "Are you scared of me?"

She leaned into him and he smiled at her small concession. "A little. I'm not hiding behind my job. I love my job."

"You're good at your job," he said, smoothing his hand over her hair. "Does this mean you wouldn't want to move to the next level?"

"Right now, I'm so exhausted, I can't think straight. Do we have to make any decisions about this now? I know that I want you and I'm not ready to let you go. Is that enough?"

"For now."

When they got to her bedroom, he helped her to the bed. "No, I want to take a bath. I feel so dirty," she said, looking up at him with pleading eyes.

"I'll help you undress and then…"

"You're not leaving," she asked. "Not after that confession about how you feel about me."

"You should rest." He wasn't made out of stone, for God's sake. If she didn't stop looking at him like that, he wasn't going to be able to leave.

"If you insist, but could you help me with my pants first?"

He gave her a wary look, but she just smiled at him. He gave in and walked into the bathroom with her. Reaching for the button on her pants, he released it and her slacks slid down her long, mouthwatering legs.

"All set?"

"Not quite," she said, softly wrapping her arms around his neck. "I don't want to bathe alone."

"I'm trying to…"

"I know and you don't have to." She pulled his shirt out of the waistband of his jeans. "Take it off."

When he complied, Sienna's hands slid over his skin. Her hands on his chest felt like two fiery brands burning his skin. He was burning up with aching need.

Her hand moved down his torso, running over the ridges of muscles along his ribs down to the thick, seriated muscle of his abdomen.

He could feel the frantic beating of her heart, her labored breathing by the quick rise and fall of her chest. He closed his eyes to better concentrate on the way her hands felt against him.

"Touch me, A.J. I want your hands on me," she demanded hoarsely.

His name on her lips uttered with such wanton need made him groan softly as he buried his face in her soft red hair. He closed his hand around her breast, his thumb brushing over the silk-clad nipple, clenching his teeth as he felt it bead under his thumb.

He filled his hands with the soft weight of her exquisite flesh, flicking his thumbs over each nipple, liking her soft gasp each time he did it.

He jerked her toward him and stripped off her bra. Her hands flew to his shoulders, her fingers digging into his flesh. She gasped when he captured a taut swollen nipple, sucking hard and urgently, moaning again when she arched her back in response to his hot mouth. His tongue teased each nipple into throbbing, aching buds.

His lips sought her mouth, sought it in a mindless search. He kissed her with ravenous demand. The sensation was sucking him into a turbulent maelstrom of spinning, whirling need, a dark realm of bliss. A tight knot of heat coiled low in his belly where his swollen flesh met hers. He moved against her, unable to withstand the urgent need inside him. With each driving thrust of his powerful hips, the heat escalated.

He picked her up and carried her to the edge of the tub, setting her down into the smooth curving indentation that would cradle their bodies perfectly.

The warm water flowed over his heated skin. She slipped off his lap and knelt between his legs running her hands along his inner thighs.

A.J.'s breath hissed in and then he moaned deep in his chest as pleasure ran like quicksilver along his shaft when Sienna took him into her soft moist mouth.

Arching his hips uncontrollably in a primitive movement, her touch was driving him to the edge of ecstasy.

He groaned as she encircled the head of his swollen shaft with the tip of her tongue.

He thought he was going to explode as the water, like a shimmering liquid rainbow, lapped gently around their heated bodies.

She rose and with slow enticing movement, climbed onto his lap, kneeling over his throbbing hardness. With slow, heated movements, she teased him with her succulent moistness, the tightly clustered curls brushing sensually against him.

Unable to stand the compelling seductive assault, A.J. shifted restlessly, his hands on her hips, his fingers digging rhythmically into her soft moist flesh. He dropped his head back, breathing hard. She moved wantonly against him again, and a low moan escaped him.

Slowly she was losing more of herself to him. Bit by tiny bit, he was taking everything she had to give him and still it amazed her how much more she wanted to give.

With a quick lithe movement, he grabbed her hands and twined them around his neck as his very blue, very hot eyes blazed into hers with such hunger and sensual intensity that Sienna ached to feel his chiseled lips on hers. She didn't have to wait long. He jerked her against him with such power that the force of it wrung a cry of surprise out of her. Without giving her a chance to even think, his lips descended to hers, fiery and demanding, as if his very life depended on her response. She reveled at the feel of the heated bare flesh of his sleek chest against her own naked skin. Her breath was dammed in her lungs and the hard pressure of his mouth sent delicious sensations to pool with hot tingles in her lower body.

She wanted more, felt as if she couldn't possibly get close enough to him. She was only aware of him and nothing else.

His hand slid over her buttocks, holding her in place as he pushed against her softness, kneading the firm curves while he pulled her tighter to him. And Sienna stilled suddenly, her breath caught between breathing in and breathing out as she felt the hot rigid length of him pressed against her.

Unable to help herself, her hands went to the part of him that was quintessentially male. With the flat of her hand she pressed against him, then cupped him, squeezing gently. It was so arousing to touch a man like this.

A full-throated groan escaped A.J.'s lips as he abruptly stopped. Sienna could feel the coiled need in him as he strained to hold on to his self-control. She felt the quivers throughout his body as he tried to master his raging desire, and she felt him lose the battle with himself. He gripped her buttocks tighter and drove himself upward, grinding his hips against her hands and stomach.

She gasped and twisted in response to the glorious feel of his hard-muscled frame.

His thighs were solid and powerful flush up against hers, his chest was unyielding, like rock.

Sienna was caught in the mindless rapture and at the desperate urging of his hands, she raised her hips and sank down onto his burning shaft. She took him deep inside her, crying out with gratification as she felt a powerful tenseness tighten with each stroke as she frantically glided over him.

She moved against him in wild abandon, drawing him in deeper and deeper, her motion faster and faster.

A.J. growled savagely as he plunged into her. She yielded, her body going soft and willing as she arched frantically to fill the empty space between them. Water sloshed against the soft pink marble lip of the tub from A.J.'s frantic movements.

She tightened around him, her legs wrapping around his hips, giving him better access. The movement was almost more than she could bear, the pressure sweet agony.

She reached up and cupped his strong jawline, running her hands over the planes of his handsome face.

Water streamed underneath her fingertips, dripping off his chin. She lapped it up with her tongue.

Her fingers left his face and traced over the taunt muscle of his biceps. He was built like a marble statue, but he was living breathing flesh, perfect in symmetry, exquisite in form.

His body tightened and released, and her name—drawn out in a long moan—burst from his throat. Sienna clung to him, holding him so tightly that she could barely breathe as air gusted in out of his lungs like a bellows. She felt like glittering sunshine, like a burst of white-hot light.

A.J. cradled her against his chest. After long moments he was finally able to speak, "Let's get you out of here and into bed."

Feeling languid and thoroughly exhausted, she went along with him.

When they were situated in bed, A.J. reached up to turn off the light.

"Leave it on," she requested, getting a full view of the scars on his back. "I'm not ready to sleep yet."

He stilled when her hand settled against the skin of his back. She wanted to soothe him even though the horror was far away in the past.

"Was it awful?" she asked.

He didn't even pretend that he didn't know what she was talking about. "Worse than that."

"Do they bother you at all?"

"No, I'm all healed," he said. "Except..."

"What?"

"I'm not as fast as I was before the blast."

"How can you be sure about that?"

"I know my body and although I've worked hard to regain my flexibility and strength, it's different, weaker."

"That takes a lot of courage to admit. Can you tell me what happened?"

"I can't give you the particulars of the mission, just that a tango—that's the enemy—was able to lob a grenade." He leaned back into the pillows and the air he stirred made her shiver, his delicious male scent driving her wild.

"What would you have done if you couldn't have gone back to the SEALs?"

"I probably would have become a trainer," he said quietly.

"Not being a SEAL...I mean..." She trailed off.

There was something about this man that robbed her of her remoteness. It was an intangible thing she couldn't put her finger on. He lived life to the fullest, sometimes on the edge, but to the fullest. She couldn't seem to get enough of absorbing all that intense energy.

He smiled. "I wouldn't shrivel up and die if I couldn't be a SEAL. The job means a great deal to me, but it's more important to contribute and be proactive, not lament about what you can't do, but what you can do."

He snuggled her against his chest, wrapping his arm around her. His scent was overpowering, shutting out all other thoughts but him. His eyes were restless, thick-lashed blue pools that locked on to hers.

"You know what I learn every time I go on a mission?" he said, a darkness shadowing his eyes, his voice hushed.

She looked at him expectantly, imagining him in camouflage, carrying a weapon, his sure strides, the confident way he held himself. She felt strange then, a savage, tender feeling that she had never felt before for a man she barely knew. She admired him. The scars evidently showed what the man was capable of.

"I learn that you have to live every single minute. I've come close to death. Very close, Sienna. I know I want to live for every minute I have."

Her eyes searched his compelling face. "Then why do you do it?"

"Because for me, Sienna, that's living." He turned onto his side to face her. "What about you and your job?"

"What about it?"

"It takes up most of your time. So much so that you don't have time for something as important as your sister's wedding."

"That bust this weekend was part of a four-month sting operation that got a dangerous drug dealer off the San Diego streets."

"And would it have gone off without a hitch if you'd been absent?"

"Well, yes, but I was part of the team. I had a right to participate."

"I'm not saying that you didn't, but where does your family fit into your life?"

"They fit," she insisted.

It wasn't long before the exhaustion of the day caught up with him and he drifted off to sleep. But Sienna lay there thinking about his question. Where did her family fit into her life?

THE WAIL OF sirens in the distance caused Sienna to come abruptly awake. A.J. was a warm wall of muscle, pressed against her from shoulder to thigh. Waking up in the middle of the night and having another human being to keep the loneliness at bay felt so damn good.

She'd thanked him for saving her life. She sat on the edge of the bed and watched him sleep, a man who affected her like no other. A one-night stand who had turned into something…more. She had been truthful when she'd told him that she wasn't ready to let him go. But would it be foolish on her part to continue to see him and have to handle the heartache later on? His and her own. She hadn't missed the rush of emotion in his eyes. It warmed her deep inside to know that she mattered to him.

A silly dare with two friends to blow off steam had

complicated her life to the nth degree. She wondered how her friends were faring with their intended targets. Wondered how they were sleeping at night.

She didn't think of A.J. as a target anymore. She couldn't think of him as anything except what he was: a compassionate man who loved his brother, his parents and his country.

With the cover of darkness, she could admit to herself that wanting him to love her wasn't foolish or reckless. Wanting him to make a commitment to her like Michelle was making to her fiancé, Geoff, wasn't foolish, either. It seemed right and possible.

Except commitment was something alien to her and maybe that was why she craved it and feared it. If commitment could be given, it could be taken away. Yet it seemed like such a strong, permanent word. A word she'd love to add to her vocabulary if she had the courage to reach out for it.

Wanting someone to love her made her think of lying awake at night, as a kid, in some other family's home because they'd never been her own. That had hurt so very much and each subsequent removal had made her close off her heart to any more pain. Before the Thompsons, she never got attached to anything. Not her room or her bed or even the family pets. They were just temporary.

And that was why permanence meant so much to her. She'd lived with temporary, the unsettling feeling of not knowing what she could depend on, and it was something she refused to ever feel again.

8

THE SOUND OF the apartment door opening woke Sienna. She got out of bed and threw on a bathrobe and grabbed her spare Glock in the drawer of her nightstand. Glancing at the clock, she saw that it was nine o'clock in the morning.

Already awake and out of bed, A.J. pulled up his jeans. They both moved silently to the hall where Sienna gave a quick peek around the corner.

"In the kitchen," she whispered.

A.J. nodded. Sienna moved away from the doorjamb and walked on silent feet to the entrance to the kitchen. She whipped around the corner and said, "Freeze."

Her mother swung away from the refrigerator door, throwing up her hands. The carton of eggs she'd been about to put into the fridge fell to the floor.

"Sienna, you scared the daylights out of me."

Sienna lowered the gun. "Lynne, I told you it wasn't necessary to shop for me." The humor was not lost on Sienna.

"Dear me." Her mother put her hand flat against

her chest. She shot A.J. a curious look and then looked back at Sienna.

"Lynne, this is Lieutenant A. J. Camacho. A.J., this is my foster mother."

"Nice to meet you. I'll just go put a shirt on." He left the kitchen.

Sienna engaged the safety and set her gun on the counter. She moved forward to help her mother sit down in a kitchen chair.

"That's quite a formidable young man, Sienna."

"You have no idea." Sienna said as she sat next to her mother. "I'm sorry I scared you."

"No. I should have called, but I thought you'd be at work." Her mother saw the bandage on Sienna's arm. "What happened? Are you all right?"

"Got in a tussle with a burly guy. He lost."

She reached out and pulled Sienna into an embrace. "Well, I'm sure glad he did and that you're fine. And the handsome lieutenant?"

"We're working together on a case."

She held her breath as her foster mother contemplated that. "Intriguing," she finally said, giving Sienna a smile that told her that Lynne knew the score. She wasn't going to stick her nose in any further.

"Actually, I am glad I had a chance to talk to you," Lynne said as she went to the counter and picked up a roll of paper towels and began to clean up the egg mess. "Your sister is pretty upset."

"I know. I'm working straight-out with this case and others are waiting for my attention."

"Honestly, Sienna you've missed the last three fittings. How are you going to get it done in time? Your sister's wedding is this weekend."

"I'll make an effort to do it in the next couple of days."

"It's already Wednesday. Time is running out."

"I know. I promise I'll make time."

"Good. Call your sister and tell her that. She thinks you don't want to be in the wedding."

"I want to be in the wedding. Why does she say that?"

"You're asking the wrong person. Now the other matter I wanted to talk to you about is dinner. It has been months. You must come on Sunday." The tough set of Lynne's jaw was a good indication that Sienna had better say yes.

"I don't have a conventional job."

"I know that, but you can take time out to eat with your family. Dad has a new toy he wants to show you."

Sienna smiled. Scott was a riot when he had something new. Using it every chance he got, making them break out in laughter when he would say, "I can fix that."

"He got a new jigsaw and he's happily building tables with it. His hobby has turned into a little business. Several of the neighbors have seen the table he built for me and they want one. Now he's commissioned for two.''

''Scott never took to retirement very well,'' Sienna said.

''No. He didn't. So we can expect you. I'm cooking roasted chicken with the works.''

''Corn bread stuffing?'' she asked hopefully.

''Of course, your favorite.'' Lynne reached out and squeezed Sienna's arm.

''I'll be there.''

Lynne's smile grew wide. ''That's fine. Oh, bring A.J. with you.''

''I don't think he…'' Sienna started to help him by getting him out of dinner with her family.

''I'd love to come,'' A.J. interrupted from the doorway, matching Lynne's smile with one of his own.

''That's settled,'' Lynne said picking up her purse from the counter. ''I trust you can get the rest of the groceries in the fridge. You might want to pick up some more eggs.''

Sienna laughed.

''I also brought over my Alfredo and a meat loaf, so enjoy.''

Her mother exited out of the apartment.

''I'm sorry about that.''

''What? The dinner invitation or the very awkward way of meeting your mother?''

''Both,'' Sienna said and laughed.

''I'd love to see your father's jigsaw.''

"If you come to dinner, believe me, you won't be able to get out of it."

"I think I might like to be invited to dinner on a regular basis."

She stopped walking away from him at that comment. Turning around she studied him. "You would?"

"Is there a problem with that?"

"No," she smiled. "My family is really nice."

"So, you're adopted?"

"I was orphaned, then I was fostered. My parents died when I was five and I was shuffled through the system more than I can count. Just when I'd get settled, I'd get pulled out and put into another home. Lynne and Scott are my seventh set of foster parents."

"Shuffled around. That must have been tough for you."

"It was hell, to be frank, but that's all in the past. I'm grounded now. A San Diego police officer and I don't have to do anything I don't want to do anymore. Speaking of my job, we'd better get going."

"We should. It can't hurt to have a quick bite and head out in about an hour."

His face was so earnest, so tender, the comment made her smile.

He was no man for her to fall in love with. He tempted her and teased her, seduced her into letting go of everything that comprised her life. He interrupted her routine. He challenged her rules and regulations, made his own kind of reality.

A seductive one.

It wasn't something she could embrace. She had her plan and it didn't include a dedicated Navy SEAL. But as she thought of the time they had spent together in her bed, she couldn't think of a single need he hadn't met. He had offered her more than his body. He had offered tenderness, comfort, his strength.

The phone shrilled and Sienna picked it up.

"Hello," she said into the receiver.

"Sienna, are you all right? Hobart said you'd taken down gunrunners and you were bleeding."

The concern in Kate's voice made Sienna smile. "I'm fine."

"Don't say it's just a scratch," Kate scolded.

Sienna pulled at a loose thread on the arm of the couch, lowering her voice a little bit more. "It is, though." Both women laughed.

"Yeah, sure. You work too hard, Sienna."

"This case can't wait," Sienna said. "I expected you to call last night. Didn't Hobart tell you what I wanted?"

There was a long pause. "Yes, but I've been jumping through hoops for St. James. I did manage to get the request to the FBI. They said they couldn't promise anything."

Sienna could detect the stress in her friend's voice. "Is everything all right?"

Kate's sigh was filled with more than just frustration. "Some old case that's causing him some indigestion. He thinks I messed up."

"Did you?"

"Who, me?" Kate snorted. "No way. He's wrong."

Sienna felt a sudden overprotective feeling for Kate who had the sweetness of a lady and a spine of steel. "You tell St. James to play nice or I'll come over there and kick his butt."

"Not exactly a good way to start seducing a guy."

Sienna shifted the phone to her other ear "How goes it?"

"Not too good."

"We'll have to work on that. When do you think you can get me the information about the guns?" Sienna hated to push when Kate was overwhelmed, but she needed that information as soon as possible.

"Tomorrow morning?"

"I have court in the morning, dammit. Just put it on my desk as soon as you can."

"And I expect a full accounting of what's going on with you when I see you. I've got to get going or I'll be late for work. Be careful with this case and with that Navy SEAL."

"I will."

Sienna dropped the receiver into the cradle. Too late. Careful had gone out the window a long time ago. She was heading straight into a whirling storm of emotion and heartache and couldn't seem to help herself or slow her crazy descent.

"What's the ETA on the gun info?"

"The FBI has the request and they said they would rush it," Sienna said.

"When did she think they'd have the data?" he asked, sitting down next to her, the scent of him heady first thing in the morning.

"She thinks tomorrow."

He scowled, reaching out and casually running his warm, calloused palm along her leg as if it was the most natural thing to do. "I was hoping for some answers sooner than that."

"So was I."

"What's the agenda for today?"

"We still have the truck we can track. I also want to find out what's holding up the M-16 serial number and the identification of the prints that were found in the truck."

"You don't give an inch, do you?" he said, a hint of amusement in his voice.

"No," she replied staring at him. "So, do you need to go home and change?"

"No, I always keep my duffel in the trunk of my car, then I'm always ready at a moment's notice."

"To leave." A cold feeling started in the pit of her stomach and branched out like killing frost. The silence stretched and Sienna looked away. It really wasn't her place to say anything to him about his lifestyle. He wasn't her man, just a temporary lover. Sienna fought for equilibrium. "You'd better hightail it down there and get your stuff. I'll make some breakfast. I think I still might have some eggs in the back of the fridge."

He nodded, got up and grabbed his keys. He put on his shoes and quietly slipped out her apartment door.

After the impromptu visit from her mother, A.J.'s words from last night came back to her. How did her family fit into her life? It wasn't until he'd voiced those words that she began to think about all the times that she had canceled because of her job. She shrugged off the unsettling feeling in the pit of her stomach. She had made an effort to fit her family in her life. A.J. barely knew her, she tried to tell herself, but a little voice jeered at her that maybe he knew her better than she knew herself.

She walked over to her purse and dug around inside. She found the receipt for the dress she'd purchased at Caroline's Bridal Shop. Walking back into the kitchen, she picked up her phone and dialed. It took her less than a minute to make another fitting appointment. See, she knew how to fit her family into her life. It wasn't difficult.

After that she dialed her sister's work number.

"Hello."

"Michelle, it's Sienna."

"Oh, hi."

"You still mad?"

"I'm working myself down to disgruntled."

Sienna smiled. "You never could stay mad at me for very long."

"No, I couldn't. Did you make another appointment?"

"Did it a minute ago."

"And you're still going to make the rehearsal dinner on Friday?"

"It's on my calendar in red ink."

"Good. I guess I can forgive you, then. When is your appointment?"

"One-thirty tomorrow."

"I'll meet you there. We can have a quick cup of coffee."

"Sounds good."

Sienna hung up the phone with a sense of satisfaction. There, she could do it. Not only did she reschedule her appointment, but she talked to her sister and smoothed things over.

A.J. came back into the apartment and Sienna looked around the doorway of the kitchen so that she could talk to him. "There are towels in the closet next to the bathroom door."

"Thanks. Sienna…" He walked toward her and stopped a few feet from her.

"How do you like your eggs?" she asked, desperate to change the subject to get away from her uncharacteristic comment about him leaving. She didn't know where that had come from.

"Scrambled," he replied with an exasperated voice.

She turned away and went into the kitchen, but he followed her.

"I haven't been able to stop thinking about what you said yesterday. I don't know where we're going to go, but just for the record, I like you a hell of a lot, Sienna."

She exhaled unevenly, trying desperately to keep her emotions tightly concealed and failing. "I like you, too," she said, a lump forming in her throat. "But we have to be realistic. There are so many reasons that it would be difficult for us. We both have demanding jobs. I don't think I'd do well with a man who's gone most of the time. A relationship worth having is one that you can build on. How can we do that if you're absent?" She raised her face and forced a smile. "It's getting late. Go take your shower, so that we can get going."

"You seem to have a lot of reasons, but I don't want to stop seeing you." He released a heavy sigh and gave her shoulder an acknowledging squeeze. He backed off and she breathed a little easier.

Entering the kitchen, she walked to the coffee-maker and switched on the machine.

She went to the refrigerator and opened the door and just stood there. Maybe it was her brush with death yesterday, but she was feeling decidedly fragile today.

A swell of emotion blindsided her. It was typical of Lynne to do this. Sienna should be accustomed to it by now, but she felt tears gathering at the back of her eyes. She loved her parents, so why did she find it so difficult to show it?

"Are you expecting something to jump out at you?"

The deep sound of his voice jerked her out of her emotional state. She avoided his gaze as she gathered her composure. Keeping her voice light, she replied, "No, it's just so full of food."

A quick glance at his face showed her the wicked grin she knew was there. He folded his arms and leaned into the doorjamb. "Correct me if I'm wrong, but that's the purpose of that particular appliance."

"Ha. Ha," she said as her voice cracked. She squeezed her eyes shut, releasing the tightness in her chest, letting it wash away a familiar and routine response.

A.J. sobered. "Are you all right?"

Sienna juggled the eggs and the package of bacon and turned to face him, a witty comeback on her tongue. That was when she got the full view of him and the eggs slid out of her hands, dropping to the floor unnoticed.

A.J. stood in the doorway dressed in just a white towel, one that barely covered all the important parts—the taut curve of his buttocks and rangy, powerful muscles of one thigh. Every line of his body flowed into the next, every delineation of muscle seemed the perfect balance of power and leanness, every flat plane solid and strong. The black silken thickness of his hair clung to the strong column of his neck as rivulets of water traveled enticingly over his taut bronzed skin.

"Does dropping eggs on the floor run in the family?" he asked. He walked into the kitchen, grabbed a paper towel and bent down to sop up the egg mess. The towel around his lean waist split even wider as his whipcord thigh muscles bunched.

"Why aren't you dressed?" she asked. It was so much easier for her to focus on his physique than to think about the turbulent emotions she was desperately trying to keep at bay.

"I couldn't find a razor. I must have left mine at home."

She set the bacon on the counter, leaned down and took the soiled paper towel out of his hand. She threw it in the trash and grabbed his hand. Leading him back to the bathroom, she pulled open the vanity door and rummaged around inside.

She emerged with the razor and very gently pushed on his shoulders until he sat on the commode, propped up by the wall behind him. Boldly, she straddled his lap, wringing a groan out of him at the suddenness of her groin pressed to the heat of his.

From out of the brown case sitting on the lip of the sink, she grabbed a can of shaving cream. She put a large dollop in her hands, rubbed it between her palms and applied the creamy lotion to his cheeks and neck. She rinsed her hands, picked up the razor and pressed the blade against his cheek. With a slow slide of the blade, she whisked off a swath of dark stubble.

A.J.'s hands came up to her shoulders and pushed her robe off, revealing the lacy teddy beneath. She shrugged out of the sleeves and let it fall to the floor. Using her finger, she tipped his chin up, placing the blade along the thick column of his throat, fascinated at the wildly beating pulse there. A smooth flick of her wrist and the whiskers were gone. She turned to rinse the razor in the sink, her lace-clad breasts sliding over the expanse of his chest.

He closed his eyes and groaned. His cock jumped and swelled beneath her.

He reached up and slipped the straps of the teddy off her shoulders. Deliberately she leaned in, the tight points of her aching nipples pressed against the hard wall of muscled torture. She leaned one way, sliding her flesh against his, getting a band of stubble just under her ear. Sliding to the other side, she repeated the action with the razor.

She reached up to grab at the washcloth on the rack above his head and he took the opportunity to strip her of the teddy. His big hands slid down over the indentation of her waist, lingering on her hips, and cupping the firm globes of her buttocks.

She leaned over the sink and wet the washcloth. Turning, she sank down on top of him, his finger sliding into her. She shuddered around his hand, gasping softly as she pressed the hot cloth to his skin and wiped off the residual shaving cream from his face.

With his free hand on her lower back, he arched her back and very slowly closed his mouth over the aching tip of her breast. She bowed into him, crying out at the hot, moist feel of his tongue.

He stood, setting her down, a slow, silky slide of his hard naked skin against her own. She gasped at the delicious feel of him, as he echoed the sound.

She trembled while the delicious weakness flooded through her. He pulled her against him.

Sienna closed her eyes, breathing in his scent, thinking there wasn't a more wonderful smell on earth. She opened her eyes and looked at him; her pulse turned thick and heavy. What she saw there was purely male, arousing and needful. He stared at her and that tender weakening stole over her bit by debilitating bit.

When he spoke, his voice came out low and strained. "You make me crazy."

She wasn't going to delude herself. She realized that something had changed. He hadn't made any promises or said anything about permanence, and she certainly wasn't going to make a fool out of herself.

With the release of tension came a flood of raw emotion that swelled in her chest. This she could do. Without taking her eyes from his, she put her own vulnerability on the line.

She reached down and skimmed his hard hip, moving her hand to gently cup his hardness. With a soft groan, he pushed himself against her hand, hardening with each stroke she gave him.

The passion in his eyes was stark and humbling, and she had to look away. She looked down at his heavy arousal and felt the heat intensify in her. Her eyes moved back to his face, and she reached up and cupped his smooth cheeks in her hands. "Let's see if I can drive you wild," she said as she watched him swallow hard and close his eyes.

She kissed each side of his mouth, tracing his lips with her tongue.

She slid her hands off his cheeks along his jaw into the strands of his dark hair, rubbing the silky mass against her fingers.

With her hands cupped around the back of his neck, she pulled him closer and sank her face into his hair.

He gasped, a quick pleasure-filled intake of breath, as her teeth sank into his skin. He groaned when her tongue came out to glide along the flesh she'd just abused.

She kissed her way along the curve of his neck and shoulder, moving down his sleek chest. When she reached the hard point of his male nipple, she laved her tongue over the tightness. He groaned, his hands rubbing up and down her back.

Her need to pleasure this man was an all-consuming ache. His hands came up, leading her mouth to his in a searing, paralyzing kiss that made her knees weak. Her hands tested the hard ropey muscles of his back, sliding over the raised scars, falling to the taut skin of his buttocks.

She opened her mouth wide against his, drinking in the unique male taste of him. Leaning heavily into him, she slid down his body until she was on her knees in front of him.

Her hands traveled down over the thick muscles of his thighs to behind his knees. He made a low, guttural sound and grasped her head, his fingers snagging in her hair, holding her when her lips grazed his hip.

She could hear the wind pick up outside. Hear the rain begin to drum against the window with a heavy force. A loud clap of thunder boomed once, then twice.

When she took him into her mouth, he jerked, staggering back until he was against the bathroom wall.

Moments, only moments later he pulled her away, his eyes gone glassy with desire. His chest heaved and they stared at each other, dark green into cobalt blue.

She pressed herself violently against him, her arms coming tight around his neck, her breathing harsh and out of control. "Take me to bed," she demanded huskily.

He picked her up and moved toward the bedroom, throwing her down on the mattress, his voice low and raw in her ear. "I need you, Sienna."

He fumbled with the packet and then his hot body was over her, and his burning flesh was inside her. Sienna could only cry out with him and sink down into their mutual hunger, igniting fires burning out of control.

AT THE DIVISION, Sienna dumped her purse in her locker and snapped the lock closed. A.J. was seated beside her desk looking over the inventory of the guns discovered at Rojas's along with the serial numbers. A note from Kate was attached to the paperwork that said, "Surprises abound. The FBI came through."

"So does Rojas's arrest help us at all?" A.J. asked, indicating the paperwork.

"No, all the guns recovered from Rojas had been part of the hijacking in Colorado. Although we have a nice solid case against Rojas for the crime, it's not going to lead us any closer to your brother."

She looked through the material on her desk. "It's not here?"

"What?"

"The FBI still hasn't run the serial number from the automatic weapon we took off Tyrone. Not to mention, I don't have a report on the fingerprints Kate got off the truck."

Sienna sat down and dialed Kate, who told her that was all she'd gotten so far.

Sienna then dialed the FBI field office. Again she was referred to the lab and again they put her on hold.

Finally someone came back on the line. "Sorry to keep you waiting, Detective. Yes, your serial number went to the home office yesterday."

"How is it I still don't have a report regarding that serial number, yet you processed a rush request for me?"

"I'm sorry, but that's all I have on my log. Perhaps you could call the home office?"

He gave her the number and she jotted it down. "Now what about my fingerprints?"

"Please hold again."

Sienna looked at A.J. and rolled her eyes.

The man came back on the line. "Detective, that request was erroneously filed and hasn't gone to the home office yet. We'll send it out right away."

"This is the second request from an ongoing case that has been botched. Can you give me an explanation for that?"

"No, ma'am, only we process so much information that sometimes things fall through the cracks. Sorry."

Sienna hung up the phone. She turned to A.J. while she dialed the FBI home office in DC. "Remember when I told you that I don't believe in coincidences?"

"Yes."

"Well, I find it strange that they could do a rush

job on hundreds of guns, yet one little serial number is overlooked.''

Sienna asked for the appropriate department. She was connected to another lab with another apologetic employee.

''No, ma'am, we don't have the request. There's no record the field office in San Diego sent it.''

She hung up and dialed the number and when she got the lab it was the same story. Although the guy was contrite and promised to look into it, Sienna's senses were tingling.

''What is that agile brain working on?''

''I feel like I'm getting the runaround and it makes me wonder why.''

''Someone doesn't want us to know where the M-16 came from or want us to confirm that David drove the truck.''

''Right, but why?''

''That's what we have to find out.''

''We could track the truck plate through DMV, which would be a place to start. Right now, I'm fresh out of ideas.''

''Let's go with that. We'll at least see where the truck came from.''

After requesting the information, they found out that the truck was registered to the naval base on Coronado.

''Interesting.'' Sienna said, ''Not really surprising since David worked on that base.''

"True. Let's go there. I can call ahead and have someone meet us to answer our questions."

THEY PULLED UP to the gate of the naval base after crossing the long, blue bridge to the island of Coronado. The guard saluted A.J. smartly. After A.J. flashed his ID and Sienna showed him her badge, the guard waved them through. A.J. drove toward the building that housed security.

They parked and got out. A.J. could smell the ocean along with diesel fuel used to run the big ships that transported the very weapons in question along with items for the exchange where navy personnel bought their groceries and sundries.

Inside the building, they walked to the front desk. Sienna showed her badge. "We're here to ask some questions regarding Corporal Buckner."

After waiting for fifteen minutes, a tall man dressed in civilian clothes approached them. "Lieutenant Camacho, Detective Parker, I'm Rob Norton, agent with the NIS—Naval Intelligence Service. Could you come with me?" He led them to a room that looked very similar to the interrogation rooms at the division. He sat down in the spare chair in the spartan room.

"What can I do for you?"

A.J. spoke. "We've got reason to believe that one of your trucks was involved in gunrunning."

"What is the basis for this assumption?"

"Detective Parker has in custody an M-16 that was

confiscated from a civilian who says he tried to buy a whole shipment of arms from Corporal David Buckner.''

''While it's true that the corporal has been listed as UL, we don't have any reason to suspect that he was involved in any other crimes. At least, at this time.''

''The perp identified David's picture.''

''As you know, Detective, perpetrators of such crimes lie to the police all the time.''

''Are you actively searching for Corporal Buckner?''

''We've got a couple more pressing cases at this time.''

''Are you involved in tracking him down?''

''No. He's not one of my cases. Is there anything else I can help you with?''

''We'd like to question Corporal Buckner's supervisor and partner.''

''I'll see what I can do.''

Rob got up and left the room.

A.J. turned to Sienna. ''What do you think?''

''I think he's lying through his teeth.''

''Yeah, I caught that.''

After thirty minutes Rob returned. ''David's supervisor can see you.''

Sienna got up from her chair. ''I don't appreciate being jerked around.''

''Beg your pardon?''

"You know what I'm talking about. You might be an NIS agent, but there's still something called obstruction of justice. I can arrest you for that and throw your ass in jail."

He gave her a smug look. "You'd have to prove that I was in some way obstructing your case."

"The navy sent me a liaison. That means they are willing to cooperate with me. Why aren't you?"

His eyebrows rose as if he was surprised that she made such an allegation. "I'm sorry that you feel that I'm being uncooperative. I assure you that your accusations are unfounded."

She brushed past him and out the door. "In a pig's eye."

"I hope you find your brother, Lieutenant."

Sienna stopped and A.J. bumped into her. She turned to the man and faced off with him. "If you don't have any connection to Buckner's case, how do you know that A.J. is his brother?"

"Must have picked it up when I was being briefed. Have a nice day."

9

―――――――

"CAPTAIN LEVINE is expecting you. Go right in." The soft-spoken civilian receptionist said.

They entered the captain's office. Captain Levine was large, hearty, with iron gray hair and a firm jaw.

A.J. came to attention. The captain eyed first Sienna and then him.

"As you were, Lieutenant," he said to A.J., nodding to Sienna. "Detective Parker."

He indicated two seats and both of them sat.

"We're here to ask some questions about Corporal David Buckner." Her tone was soft but still forceful.

"Buckner's officially been listed as UL, but I'm inclined to cut the kid some slack. There's no finer Marine." He sat back in the chair, bringing with him a letter opener shaped like a sword. He drew the blade through his fingers.

"A truck from your base was discovered in downtown San Diego. I have a statement from a witness that said that Buckner was selling guns out of the back of that truck." Sienna said, her eyes following the way he was petting the blade.

"You think he's involved in illegal actions. Don't

buy it." His eyes shifted toward Sienna and A.J. thought for a moment that the man looked nervous.

"You're in charge of security. Did you have reports that a truck is missing?" she said, sitting forward in her chair.

"No, no one has reported that. Maybe you could call my receptionist with the information and I'll track it here." His eyes shifted away from her and focused once again on the sword in his hands. "You could talk with his partner." The captain's eyes twisted to A.J. "What is your part in this investigation, Lieutenant?"

"I've been assigned as navy liaison."

The captain's eyebrows rose.

"We'd like to talk to Buckner's partner," Sienna said, rising.

A.J. had been in the military long enough and been through enough covert operations that he was well aware when someone was being tightlipped about classified information. Captain Levine had that look.

"My receptionist can lead you to Sergeant Gibson," he said, nodding to them.

The dispatcher at the security desk called in Gibson. A.J. and Sienna were taken back to the same room where they'd talked to Norton. They sat down in the nondescript gray metal chairs.

A man was ushered into the room. He stood at attention.

"Sergeant Gibson reporting as ordered, sir."

A.J. could see his name printed on his uniform. Gibson was a tall, muscular black man with a shaved head and kept his eyes straight ahead. He was wearing cammies with the sleeves rolled up. The uniform was impeccably clean and pressed.

Sienna piped up. "Detective Parker from SDPD and this is Lieutenant Camacho. We need to ask you a few questions about Corporal Buckner."

"Yes, ma'am." Sergeant Gibson said, his brows narrowing.

"Do you have any idea where he might be?" Sienna asked in her no-nonsense detective voice.

"No, ma'am." Sergeant Gibson said, sweat beginning to glisten off his smooth skull.

"Would you know anything about a stolen military truck filled with guns?" Sienna persisted.

"No, ma'am," he said a little too quickly.

A.J. put his hand on Sienna's arm. She was frustrated, and knew as well as he did that this guy wasn't telling them everything he knew. But badgering him wasn't going to help the case.

"David's an upstanding guy. He would want to do the right thing." The man had spoken out of turn, and for a moment A.J. saw something flash across his eyes.

"Thank you for your help," he said and weathered Sienna's glare as he dismissed the Marine. He and Sienna left the room, and exited the building. But when they reached A.J.'s car, she grabbed a fistful of his shirt.

"He's holding back. Everyone we talked to today was tap-dancing. I saw it in their faces." Her face was flushed with fury. "I hate being sandbagged."

"I know," he growled.

"Why didn't you let me interrogate Gibson some more? You ended that interview too soon. I told you I call the shots."

"Something's going on between Gibson and David, but at this point we don't know what it is or if it has anything to do with those stolen weapons."

"I can't find out if you won't let me do my job."

"Let me question Gibson alone."

"You are not running this investigation, Camacho." Ice sheathed that husky voice.

"I'm well aware of that, but I'm the navy liaison. I know that Marine would rather face a firing squad than rat out his partner. Trust me on this?" Catching her hand, A.J. closed his fist around it. So much heat and energy in that one small hand radiating into him.

"Trust? You think I don't trust you?"

"I think you have it in the back of your mind that I'm David's brother and I want to keep him safe."

"You do. Don't deny it."

"I'm not, but I promised you that I would be objective."

"Yes, you did and I see your point. I know all about protecting your partner and I understand Gibson's reluctance to get Buckner in trouble,'' she said, taking a determined step away from him.

A.J. shifted, blocking her. Not sure if he had the trust he suddenly wanted from her. Halting her quick shift away from him, he gripped her shoulders. "Do you trust me?"

For a moment she gazed up into his eyes. "Yes."

The simple answer hit him hard in the heart. It was something special to gain this woman's trust.

But although he went back inside to talk to Gibson, he had already gone off shift.

A.J. got his address from the receptionist, but there was no answer at Gibson's house.

When A.J. got back in the car, Sienna said, "I could put out an APB on Gibson."

"No," A.J. insisted, "getting hauled in by the police will only make him clam up more. I'll track him down."

THE DAY HAD PASSED and they were still no closer to finding David than they'd been that morning. The good news was that the crime scene investigation of the military truck revealed no blood on either the window shards or the seat. Yet, even with that encouraging news, A.J. couldn't seem to relax.

He paced in front of Sienna's desk while she handled a few details for another case. Several detectives eyed him with wary eyes.

A.J. rolled his shoulders trying to release some of

the tension. Sienna finished her conversation and hung up the phone. She rubbed at the back of her neck.

"A.J., let's get out of here and blow off some steam."

He nodded and followed her as she exited division headquarters. The pressure tightened inside him as they walked to the parking lot. The sky was purple and orange in the west. Lights were coming on as dusk settled into night.

"Something will break tomorrow. I can feel it."

He moved away from the car and swore.

Sienna said softly, "I think I know what you need. You still have your duffel in your trunk?

"Yeah."

"Got shorts and a T-shirt?"

"Yeah."

"Good. Follow me."

A.J. HIT THE BAG so hard, he felt as if his fist was going to come through the other side. He'd been hitting it steadily ever since Sienna had dragged him into the police gym and given him a pair of boxing gloves.

A feeling of despair washed through him and the frustration only grew deeper until he was pummeling the bag with out of control strokes.

Something tore inside him, something that had been building since he'd first heard that Sienna was looking for David. Fear. It raged at him and scored his insides, a fear he'd tried to bury.

He ran out of steam, and a hollow feeling filled him until he was clutching at the bag. Sienna was up and moving, forcing him to let go of the bag. He held on to her instead.

"I don't want to believe it. I don't want to believe that my brother could have done something illegal."

"I know."

"I'm afraid for him," he whispered against the softness of her hair.

"I know." Her hands moved up and down his back in a comforting motion.

"How am I going to tell my parents?"

"We still haven't found him, A.J. We haven't gotten his side of the story. You don't have to tell your parents anything just yet."

"It looks bad, though."

"I'd say yes, if it wasn't for all that maneuvering the navy types were doing today. Something just doesn't seem to fit, but I don't know what."

Back in the parking lot, he cupped her face between his hands before she could settle into the passenger seat. "Thanks. I was about to come out of my skin."

"I know that feeling. Punching that bag is the only thing that gets me through sometimes."

He nodded, and got into the car. When he was settled into the driver's seat, she said, "Being fit in this job may save my life one day. At the academy we had to jump these hurdles. Everyone hated them, but I loved them. I used to get ribbed all the time.''

''For training in the military, especially in the SEALS, you have to arrive in shape or you'll fail almost immediately.''

A.J. pulled up in front of a diner and they got out.

''I've heard about SEAL training and the academy is nothing compared to that. At least we got to go home for rest and relaxation. I guess you didn't get much R and R during training.''

Settling into a booth, they ordered. ''If you consider sleeping in the mud R and R, I guess I got that.''

Sienna shook her head. ''You guys are scary.''

''Not really. It's mind over matter. SEAL training disciplines you to get through so much tough stuff, missions are a piece of cake. Sloughing through mud. No problem. Staying submerged in icy water for an hour. Simple.''

''What do you think you're going to do about your diminished capacity?''

A.J. answered after the waitress set down a chicken salad for Sienna and a steak for A.J. ''You make me sound like I'm ready for the old folks' home.''

Forking up a bite, Sienna gave him a cheeky smile. ''You know what I mean. You're far from the old folks' home. Damn, A.J., you are a hunk.''

He laughed, looking down to cut his steak. The slight tinge to his skin made warmth curl inside her. He blushed. It was so sweet.

"Am I? So if I quit the SEALs I should go into modeling?"

She paused in reaching for her drink. "You'd quit?"

"If I can't perform my job 110 percent, then I don't belong on missions where peoples' lives hang in the balance," he said quietly.

"There are so many men who wouldn't admit this to themselves, let alone someone else."

"To tell you the truth, this is the first time I've said it out loud. I've been trying to deny it for a while."

"If you admit it to yourself, then you have to do something about it."

A.J. shrugged. "I learned to be honest with myself a long time ago. Sometimes it's a hard pill to swallow, but it's good medicine." A.J. threw down some bills and rose. "Let's get out of here."

Could he possibly make her admire him more? And his words about honesty made her squirm inside. She was honest with herself, she told that jeering little voice.

They exited the diner. It looked like rain was threatening again.

"Have you talked to your sister?" A.J. asked. "In case you're confused on this part, you need to contact her."

Sienna sidestepped him, amazed at his ability to see more than she wanted him to see. It was almost more unnerving than his ability to make her want him.

"I made another fitting appointment for tomorrow afternoon. So you see, I make room for my family." She told that jeering little voice to shut up.

"Making the appointment and keeping the appointment are two different things," A.J. said.

Sprinkles of rain peppered her skin. "This time I'm going."

"I can see that you're determined."

They stared at each other for a moment.

"We're standing in the rain," Sienna pointed out.

He looked up and smiled. "So we are. Isn't it great to feel the cool drops against your skin? I love rain on a mission. Not only does it shield us from enemy eyes, but the sensation of being real, concrete, gives me an edge."

He lowered his head and pressed his mouth against hers. She still marveled how his could be so soft, so clever as his lips moved over hers with a sensual, seductive slide. He cupped her cheek, moving his thumb rhythmically around her skin as if he couldn't seem to believe it was so soft.

She kissed him back because she couldn't help it. It wasn't like taking at all. It was like succumbing.

She'd been so careful for so long, she couldn't believe she was being seduced by a rogue, one she'd invited into her bed.

But invite him she had and she didn't want him to disappear out of her life, but she didn't see any way around the huge problem of his dangerous and demanding job.

"I'm getting all wet, Camacho."

He lifted his hand and smoothed it over her hair, his eyes softening to tenderness. "Live a little, Parker. It won't kill you," he whispered.

"Are you sure about that?" She pulled out of his arms and headed for the car. His talk about living brought raw emotions to the surface. Sienna didn't care for chaos, but the more she tried to order those feelings, the more they slipped through her defences.

"Living is a rush, Sienna. Taking what you want with both hands and breaking out of your safe little world feels good," he said, slipping behind the wheel.

"I like my rules and regulations. It orders my life."

"It boxes you in, too."

"Freethinking might be admired in the SEALs, but I've found that procedure works for me. It's gotten us far on this investigation."

"I can't argue with that, but that doesn't mean that some of my methods weren't effective."

He put the car in gear, pulling away from the curb. On the ride over to her apartment, she wondered if he felt as unsettled about their relationship as she did. Letting him off the hook seemed to be the best idea.

She waited until she was inside her apartment before she turned to A.J., putting her hand against his chest. "I'm not asking for any promises from you, A.J. We're clear on that score."

"I'm not good at making promises I can't keep. I wish I knew where we were going, but I don't."

"The future always takes care of itself. Why don't we just worry about the here and now?" she answered.

She gave him her honesty and felt certain that enjoying the moment with him while it lasted was all that she could do right now. Pursuing a relationship with A.J. would lead her inevitably to heartache. They were of two different mind-sets without common ground.

"Then we go on and find out."

"I guess so."

He drew her deeper into the apartment and she reveled in the predatory light in his eyes. She gasped when he swept her off her feet. "In case you didn't realize, Lieutenant, I'm a tough cop. I don't need to be carried."

He set her on the floor close to the bed. "You're lovely," he murmured, one finger outlining the skin along her collarbone.

Sienna felt hot blood rush to her face and burn. "You've obviously been on one mission too many," she replied awkwardly.

He was amused at her obvious embarrassment but declined to answer. He concentrated instead on dropping kisses lightly over her face, her forehead, her eyelids, her cheeks.

Sienna had a hard time letting her guard down, but

with A.J.'s mouth on her, she found it easy to succumb to the heightened pleasure, seduced away from caution and safety.

His hands went to her clothing. Wasting no time, he stripped her heated body, each touch of his hand making her heart beat wildly for more, each breath he took making her own breathing align with his.

She removed his clothes just as quickly, taking no time. His hot, wet mouth moved down her neck to her collarbone, gently nipping the ridge of flesh, then to her aching nipples. Everything in the world ceased to exist. There was just A.J., hot and hard, darkly seductive. A moan caught at the back of her throat, clamoring to get out. She could feel his body pulse with passion, strength, need, and she knew a wild desire to hold him in her hand, to feel the length of him, to feel him hard with the promise of sensual satisfaction.

She could feel the heat of his arousal rubbing against the apex of her thighs. He moaned softly, his intense eyes closing, his chest flattened against hers, the hard ridges of his chest a sensual goad.

The pressure of his weight was wonderful, the scent of him thick with male muskiness and arousal. She reveled in the feel of him against her.

It was sheer madness on her part as her hands stole around to his firm, muscled buttocks, sliding over the hot taut flesh to pull his hips against hers. He twisted his head to the side, his breathing catching on another

moan. His hands moved into her hair, his fists clenching and releasing to slide through the length.

He pressed his hard arousal against her belly. Nothing else mattered to Sienna at this moment, not her
loss of control, not anything. Her hands tightened on
his sleek backside, bringing him closer, wanting
more, wanting him inside her.

He looked into her eyes, studied them. "Sienna?"

In answer, her head fell back, and her lids half
closed at the warm seductive lights in his eyes. "A.J.,
I want you. I want…"

"This?" he said, his voice hitching. His head
dipped and his smooth lips sent ripples of sensation
skittering down her back, his fine white teeth nipped
her skin, and Sienna gasped as goose bumps swelled
all over her body. His warm, wet tongue stroked her
skin, and her nipples tightened into hard, heated tips.
She moaned. Her hands came up and delved into his
hair as soft as strands of hot, wet silk. Sienna gently
cupped his head as if it were the most precious thing
on the earth.

And it was.

He was.

So precious.

"Sienna, I can't get enough of you."

She saw her own hunger mirrored in his eyes. He
wanted her hunger; he wanted her so badly that she
could feel his body shudder with a keen, pulsating pain.

His demanding mouth came down on hers again, drawing a moan from deep inside her. "A.J.," she pleaded against his lips.

The passion that had been burning inside her could not be denied. His eyes were soaked in desire, glazed with need. His eyes moved with a slow, hot slide down her body. Sienna felt as if she couldn't breathe, as if suddenly her lungs had ignited and were burning. She was burning. When A.J. pressed the full length of his body against hers, the hardness of him sent a violent tremor through her.

His mouth came down on Sienna's lips. She couldn't think, couldn't reason, couldn't breathe.

Heat. Everywhere he touched her body brought scorching heat, burning within and without. A.J. shuddered with it, his body pressing deeper into hers. Sienna writhed with the intensity of that hot need in an uncontrollable movement, afraid of that heat, wanting to escape, yet oddly yearning to be consumed by it.

The feel of A.J. pressed solidly against her made her want to scream with her need for him. His breath was hot on her neck where he'd buried his face, inches away from her skin, sensitized almost to the point of insanity. His touch branded her. Beautiful, callused fingers trailed over her neck and shoulders, moved with aching slowness down the ridge of her spine where goose bumps were raised and multiplied across her skin. His hands finally spread out to loop around the flare of her naked hips.

A low sound escaped her as he pressed his hard length against her, his hips undulating with uncontrollable movement.

"Sienna," he rasped.

She twisted against him, an unvoiced cry trapped inside her as he moved his hips slowly. His mouth lowered to sweep the hollow where her neck flowed into her shoulder, his tongue moving in slow, delicious circles over her skin. Her passion came from her throat as a gasping, tearing sound of need. "A.J.," she pleaded softly.

Her breasts ached for his touch and she gasped as his hands slid up her rib cage. Her nipples were ready and erect when he finally cupped them in his big, rough, hot hands. His mouth descended to her ear, his voice straining with aching need as he bit her lobe, sending prickles of fire to the tips of her beasts. She arched into him with a moaning cry.

"Tell me what you want," he demanded, moving beyond control and dragging Sienna with him with those spoken words.

She cried out again and arched harder into him, her hands against the wall of his chest, an unmovable, burning hardness. As he took her aching nipples between his fingers, pinching and tugging on them, Sienna thought it was more than she could take. His eyes blazed with a hard, unyielding fire that reached

out and burned her. She gasped at the magnificence
of him, his dark unruly hair hanging in heavy strands
of tangled silk. She reached up and ran her fingers
through it, and he closed his eyes as if in agony.

His mouth descended and captured hers, his lips
demanding her to surrender, to submit to him, to give
him all that she had to give. Sienna couldn't give any
less.

She had been made for him. "I want you inside
me, A.J."

As he lifted her easily, his biceps bulging from the
weight of her, she brought her hands up to clasp his
wrists, sliding seductively over the silky hair on his
forearms until she reached the tight, round bulges.
She tested the hot, taut skin and felt the strength of
him pulsate into her fingers until the maleness of him
seemed to seep into her blood and burn.

For a moment of heated silence, he just stared at
her; then he caught a nipple between his teeth, licking
and sucking until she arched in desperate, aching
need, causing little fissions of heat to explode in her
stomach, reaching into the core of her, stabbing with
needles of pleasure so intense she was afraid she was
beginning to unravel.

"Wrap your legs around me," he ordered, his
hands moving down her body to support her, cupping
her bottom. He leaned into her, pressing her back up
against the wall. With a soft cry, she wrapped her legs
around his hips. "A.J., please."

At that moment, nothing mattered. Her world narrowed down to having him inside her. "Oh, please. Please," she sobbed with desperation and need.

With a move that showed his amazing strength, he reached down into her bedside drawer and pulled out a packet and sheathed himself.

He pushed into her, and her words ended on a deep moan. He pumped into her, drawing out of her slowly. She tightened her arms around his neck, putting her lips against his throat.

A.J.'s tempo increased until he was moving frantically in and out. Sienna clung to him incoherent and shredded with pleasure.

Sienna lost all sense of control as the pressure inside of her began to build and build, pulling into one hot, pulsating center. He moved again and again, until the myriad sensations joined into one aching spasm. She cried out and arched stiffly against him, the explosion sending her off into a shattering release. But before the first contraction finished shuddering through her, he clutched at her, and a low tormented groan ripped from him. Slowly he dropped to his knees until Sienna felt her bottom hit the floor.

She felt as if her whole body had turned to rubber. A.J.'s harsh breathing slowed to a more normal rhythm. With careful movements he stood, pulling her up with him. Warm and drowsy, he carried her to her bed, settled her on the mattress and lay down next to her. He kissed her forehead and pulled her body against his, needing to feel her hands on him.

A.J. finally became aware of Sienna's choppy breathing and rolled them both to the side, unwilling to let her go completely. He had never experienced such heady pleasure with any other woman.

His vow not to let her get too close was gone. She'd already made a foray into his heart.

He closed his eyes as his arms wound around her. He wasn't going to kid himself here; he knew there was no future for them. Sienna was wrapped up in his life right now. In the beginning, he'd joined this investigation because he'd needed her to find his brother. He'd thought this affair was going to be short and intense and then it would be over. But he had to rearrange his thoughts. How could he reorder his life to keep her in it? She wasn't someone he could leave and never see again. He was falling for her, and what made it worse, was that he knew it.

10

SIENNA STOOD at the sliding glass doors, slowly working out the kinks in her sore shoulder. She'd left A.J. peacefully asleep while she enjoyed the blue twilight of early morning. Her apartment was unnaturally quiet, the stillness adding to the twisting feeling in her chest. Folding her arms against the chill, she rested her hip against the cupboard and watched the dark brew trickle into the carafe, the burble of the coffeemaker unnaturally loud in the perfect stillness.

She felt wonderful. Everything was under control. The investigation was going to break—she could feel it—the fitting for the wedding was taken care of, and she'd settled the issue of A.J. last night.

When the coffee was done she pulled open the cupboard door and got out two mugs. She paused and looked at the two on the counter. How odd for her to take down two. It wasn't like A.J. was here to drink the coffee just yet. Funny how it seemed so natural for her to plan for him.

Was that a bad sign that she was deluding herself about how orderly everything was?

She poured herself a cup and headed for the living

room. The elated feeling wouldn't last, but she was going to enjoy it as much as she could. She was having a great fling with a great guy. She'd never had a problem letting go. When the time came, she would let go of A.J., too.

She ran into him looking deliciously sleep tousled as he grunted at her.

"There's coffee in the kitchen." She watched as he went and poured himself a cup.

Sienna heard a ringing noise, but it wasn't her phone. She followed the sound. The noise was coming from his jeans. She set her cup down on the end table and picked up the pants, digging into the pocket.

Without thinking, she flipped the phone open. "Hello."

There was silence on the other end of the line, and then a man spoke. "I'm sorry. I must have the wrong number."

"Are you trying to reach A.J.?"

"Yes, this is his father."

"Just a minute."

She went back into the kitchen where A.J. was sipping his coffee slowly at the kitchen table.

She handed the phone to him. "It's your father."

"Thanks," he said, putting the phone to his ear. "Hi, Dad."

While he was speaking to his father, Sienna went into her room to get ready for court.

A few minutes later, A.J. wandered in.

"What did you tell him?" Sienna asked, putting on a bracelet with blue stones.

"As little as possible, but my dad isn't stupid. He knows there's much more than what I'm telling him." He stared at her for a split second, and then looked away, the muscles in his jaw bunching.

She tried to clear away the sudden cramp in her throat. "It's no use telling him information we haven't verified. It will only worry him more."

Releasing a heavy sigh, she dropped her chin and looked down. He was barefoot, his feet finely formed. She moved her eyes up the expanse of his leg to the worn fly where frayed threads separated faded denim from the metal zipper teeth.

"Right. Need-to-know basis. This is going to kill him."

She went to him, wrapping her arms around his neck and holding on. "I'm so sorry." All she could do was give him her comfort.

He broke the embrace and sat down heavily on the bed. "Me, too. When my stepfather came into my life, I resented him and did everything I could to keep my distance."

"Why?" She curled her hands over his thumbs, his fingers coarse against her and oddly gentle.

"Because I was afraid that he would disappoint me. I never knew my father and didn't have any kind of role model, so it was easier to shut him out. Protect myself."

He watched her with an unwavering stare, the dark stubble accentuating the stern set of his jaw. Compelled by the pressure of his hands, she held his gaze.

"How did you get over that?"

He studied her, as if weighing her question, then closed his eyes and released his breath in a rush. One of his hands slipped to the back of her neck and he squeezed. "He never gave up. He proved himself to me countless times until finally I was worried I would disappoint him."

Caught in the spell of their fragile harmony, she found peace in the touching of bodies and hands, the comfort of connection with another human, one she didn't have to pretend with.

A.J. noticed her bracelet. "That's pretty."

"My sister gave it to me as a friendship present. I wear it when I have to face unpleasant tasks. It gives me confidence." Gently she held his face. "I have to get to court."

"I can do some recon while you're busy."

"What does that mean?" Her heart lurched. He couldn't be suggesting what she thought he was suggesting.

"SEALs have all kinds of skills and we're not shy about using them."

"What kinds of skills?" Trying to be open-minded, Sienna decided to play this out; maybe he had a different angle.

"I can get into and out of places without being

seen, part of our covert training. Taylor will never know I'm there.''

Sienna closed her eyes as if praying for divine understanding of a particularly stupid comment. When they opened she shot him a sideways look that could have etched stone. ''Are you actually standing here in front of a cop and talking about a B and E?''

''It's not like I'm going to rob the guy,'' he said indignantly. ''He's the thief. I'll just scout around.''

This was it, the difference between them. ''Absolutely not! It's against the law.''

''The guy's a known gunrunner. We have grounds for suspicion,'' he replied in exactly the same clipped tones she'd used.

''The Bill of Rights is the big deal. I took an oath and I don't intend to break it for some scum of the earth who doesn't deserve to be walking the streets. I follow the letter of the law in case that's not clear to you. If I decide we need to question him, we'll bring him in.''

''Who's going to know?'' A.J. asked.

''I'll know.'' She looked him straight in the eyes. ''You can't do it, A.J.''

His jaw clenched and he looked away from her. ''All right. We'll play it your way for now.''

She breathed a sigh of relief. ''The reason we haven't questioned him so far is that I think it would tip him off that we're looking for your brother.''

''You think he's after David?''

"Someone is. Tyrone said that the shipment belonged to Taylor. I think that it fits."

Sienna looked at her watch and realized that if she didn't get moving now, she'd be late. "I've got to make it to court on time. Believe me. A.D.A. Jericho St. James doesn't like to be kept waiting."

"How long will you be?" he asked.

"Probably all morning."

"Right."

AFTER SHOWERING and shaving, it didn't take A.J. long to get to the naval base. Gibson entered the questioning room with a wary expression on his face, but when he saw that Sienna wasn't there, he seemed to relax.

"I know that you have information about Corporal Buckner that you're not willing to tell the SDPD. How about you tell his brother?"

"I thought I recognized you," Gibson said.

"I'm here to help him."

"Sir, with all due respect, why were you with a cop, then?"

"She's point on this investigation. I'm just here to make sure my brother doesn't get hurt. If you have any information where he might have gone or what he is involved in, I need to know it."

A.J. could see the indecision on Sergeant Gibson's face. "Sir, I helped him unload a military truck and load up a U-Haul," Gibson said matter-of-factly.

A.J. had to sit down. "Did he explain?"

"No, sir. He said the less I knew the better."

"Do you know where he went?"

Gibson hesitated, conflict on his face.

"Help me, Gibson. I think David's in danger. I don't want to lose my brother."

Gibson released a pent-up breath, and said, "I saw a Nevada map on the seat of the truck with a route mapped and a city circled."

"What city?

"Lake Tahoe."

"Why did you help him, Sergeant?"

"David and I were stationed at the U.S. Embassy in Angola. When the unrest broke out over there, he saved my life along with the lives of sixty other people." Gibson looked away then back. "I should tell you that David has huge gambling debts. I offered to help him out with money, but he refused," Gibson said.

"Thank you for telling me everything."

A.J. left the security building, his gut churning. It wasn't news to him that David had unloaded that truck, but it was wrenching to actually hear that he had.

A.J. had taken the list of gunrunners from the computer search yesterday and he looked down at it now. He truly didn't want to piss Sienna off, but David's life could be hanging in the balance. He wasn't going to Tahoe until he was sure that Jack didn't have David stashed somewhere in that warehouse.

SIENNA WAITED outside the D.A.'s office. Jericho St. James had asked her to meet him after her testimony. He had a pressing matter to discuss with her.

Impatience buzzed along her nerve endings. In addition to the urgency to get those stolen guns off the street, there was the real concern about the well-being of A.J.'s brother. She could feel David's time running out.

She walked up to the young, pert receptionist sitting behind a shoulder-high counter flanked by file cabinets, telephone switchboard and computer. "How much longer will A.D.A. St. James be?"

"He called to say that he'd be here by ten o'clock."

Sienna looked at her watch. "That was ten minutes ago."

"I'm sorry, Detective, but he stressed that it was urgent that he talk to you. Can you spare a few more minutes?"

"Sure."

Jericho walked in moments later. As in court, he commanded attention the minute he entered a room. He was attractive and intelligent and Sienna could understand Kate's interest. But he was a little too intense and styled for her tastes in his charcoal gray suit coat with a red power tie, his dark hair styled to perfection.

"Sienna, sorry to keep you waiting," he said briskly as he led the way into his office.

Making herself comfortable in one of the wooden chairs in front of his desk, Sienna waited for him to settle.

He glanced at the messages on his desk, then put them aside to set his briefcase down. Sitting, he leaned back and said, "The Rojas bust was ironclad. Good police work makes my life so much easier."

"Did you bring me here to give me a compliment?" Sienna asked dryly. "A phone call would have sufficed."

Jericho smiled. "No. But it is about Rojas."

"What about him?"

"He says that he has information that your informant is part of Jack Taylor's team."

"Tyrone Knight?"

"One and the same. He says that Knight has performed contract killings for Taylor. He's willing to testify against Knight and Taylor."

"For a reduced sentence, I'm sure."

"You got it, but I can't make the deal."

"Why not?" she demanded.

Jericho picked up a pen and started tapping it against a file folder. "Comes from the D.A. I have to sit on it until next week."

"Why?"

"I was hoping you could shed some light on it. You offered Knight up as a witness to Rojas."

Sienna closed her eyes and huffed out a breath. "And immunity."

"Right, but don't get nervous. The immunity is for the gun charges. The murders are separate."

"Fat lot of good that does us. If you can't make a deal with Rojas until next week, Knight walks."

"Bingo."

"Why does the D.A. want Knight to walk?"

"He won't say. Won't even tell me who's putting pressure on him."

"The D.A. is willing to let a murderer go."

"From what I could tell, he wasn't willingly doing anything. I asked his secretary if he'd had any visitors lately and she told me that two suits had been in his office earlier that day."

"Suits? As in FBI?" Her sixth sense started tingling all over again. First she gets the runaround by the FBI; now they seemed to be directly meddling in her case.

"That would be my guess. What case are you working right now?"

"Knight failed to yield to an emergency vehicle. When he was stopped, a sharp-eyed officer saw a military weapon in plain sight in his car. Not one easily purchased at a gun store. One thing led to another and now I'm officially working with a navy liaison to track down a military policeman who might be involved in the theft of hundreds of weapons.''

''How does Taylor fit into your investigation?''

''Knight said that the MP was working for Taylor and the shipment is his.''

''Lots of connections to Taylor.''

''Right, and I don't believe in coincidences.''

''Do you have anything you can hold Knight on?''

''No.''

Jericho sighed. ''We'll have to console ourselves with Rojas for now. Hopefully we'll be able to pick up Knight again.''

A.J. WASN'T THERE. When she sat down, she found a message on her desk. It was from the cyber forensics office.

Walking through the door, she immediately headed for Gary Mancuso who was fiddling around with his keyboard. ''What do you have for me?''

Gary smiled at her from behind his wire-rimmed glasses. ''That was one toasted hard drive,'' he said as he moved from the computer he was working on to another model. ''I managed to get a few files out. Some of it is routine stuff.''

''So it's a dead end?''

''Not exactly.'' He smiled even wider. ''I was able to recover this Excel file intact.''

''What does that tell us?''

''Look for yourself.''

Sienna bent over his shoulder and gazed at the screen and her heart sank as she read the contents.

A.J. DROVE TO the warehouse where Taylor had his business. In minutes he was moving silently across the asphalt-topped roof of the warehouse and knelt to remove the access panel. Silently, he dropped into the opening.

On silent feet he made his way to the warehouse office. There were several sentries, but A.J. eluded them with ease. When he got to the glass-enclosed office, he knelt down so as not to be seen by the obviously angry man inside. He was throwing things. A.J. heard them cracking off the Plexiglas.

"Of all the incompetence. Listen to me and listen to me good. I want those guns."

"But I don't know where he is," the voice came over the speakerphone. "I tracked him to Mexico, but he changed license plates on the U-Haul to throw me off."

"I don't care—"

A.J. heard the line beep. "Wait, Ray, I have someone on the other line."

A.J. heard the voice change.

"Mr. Taylor?"

"Yes."

"Jimmy Lee Moran in Tahoe. I wanted to check with you. There's some guy here who claims to be selling a shipment of guns for you. Since you didn't contact me about the shipment, I wanted to make sure it was legit.''

"What's the guy's name.''

"Buckner.''

"This is too rich. When did Buckner contact you?''

"Just five minutes ago.''

"That's great. When did he say he could give you delivery?''

"Tomorrow.''

"Take him out for me and you can name your price for the guns.''

"That's a deal I'll take.''

"Keep me posted,'' Taylor said as he switched back to the other line.

"Listen, Ray. Jimmy just called. The bastard is in Tahoe trying to unload my guns to my clients. I want you to meet my man at the airport and fly out there.''

"What for?''

"To take care of him.''

"Why can't Jimmy do it?''

"This is extra insurance. And you're the one who hired the bastard. I want you to take care of it. No little nobody military punk is going to make me a laughingstock,'' Taylor said.

A.J. silently made his way out of the warehouse. An unsettled feeling twisted his gut. They were going to kill his brother.

WHEN A.J. WALKED into the division, Sienna rose from her desk. "Where have you been? We caught a break—''

"I know where David is. We've got to go."

"Where?"

"Tahoe."

"How did you find out he went there?"

"Taylor"

"Taylor?" She sighed deeply and grabbed a handful of his shirtfront. "I asked you not to do that." Her voice was so quiet, but deadly.

She paced away from him and came back. "Don't regs mean anything to you? You're in the navy. I can't believe this."

He grabbed her upper arms and halted her words. "I don't have time for this. They're going to kill David."

"Who?"

"Either the two guys Taylor sent to Tahoe or a client named Jimmy Lee Moran who knows that David has double-crossed Taylor. When David rendezvouses with them, they're going to kill him and take the guns."

"How long do we have?"

"Until tomorrow."

"Sienna?"

The sound of Michelle's voice drew Sienna's attention away from A.J. "Michelle? What are you doing here?"

"You had a fitting thirty minutes ago."

"Oh, God, Michelle. I'm sorry."

"If we go right now, the fitter said she could work you in."

"I can't go now."

"Why is it always the same old answer with you? Your job. It always comes first. Don't bother to get fitted. Don't bother to come at all."

"Michelle…"

Sienna ran her hands through her hair as Michelle turned on her heel and walked away.

"Sienna, I'm sorry," A.J. offered.

Sienna couldn't acknowledge the pain she was feeling. A man's life was hanging in the balance; she couldn't worry about her sister. "I'll get in contact with the Tahoe police."

"No."

"What do you mean?"

"We have to go."

"To Tahoe?"

"Yes."

"I don't have jurisdiction in Tahoe."

"Don't get the police involved, Sienna. Let me talk to him. I know I can get him to surrender."

"It's not correct procedure, A.J."

"Damn the procedure, this is David's life I'm talking about. He'll fight. Please, Sienna. I'm begging you."

"The captain won't approve it."

"We won't know that until we ask him."

In ten minutes they were in the captain's office, but as soon as Sienna made her request, Raoul shook his head.

"But it's a credible tip, Captain, that David Buckner's in Lake Tahoe," Sienna said.

"I don't doubt that. That's not the issue. We don't have jurisdiction in Tahoe. Call the police force there and let them pick him up."

"I'm going, Captain, with or without Sienna."

"It'll be without," the captain said firmly.

"I'M COMING with you."

"Captain change his mind?" A.J. jeered as he jerked open the car door and got into the driver's seat. Sienna slid into the seat next to him. He pulled his cell phone from his coat pocket and dialed a number. It didn't take him long to get the plane he needed from one of his teammates.

"Sienna—"

"I know what you're going to say. This could cost me my job." She turned to him. "But what will it cost you? I have evidence David took those weapons. He's been working for Taylor for a year."

"How do you know this?"

"We recovered an Excel file from his computer. It has details of everything. The cargo, the drop dates, the money. Everything."

A.J. closed his eyes, still holding out hope that his brother was innocent of the charges against him. How could David have changed so much and how could it have happened right under A.J.'s nose? It seemed that he didn't know his brother at all. It made him question the time he spent away from home. Question his dedication to a navy that had somehow robbed him of his brother.

"Get out."

"No, A.J. I'm coming with you. You need me. I can get information you can't."

"Sienna—"

"Just drive."

11

SMALL PLANES were *not* her thing. As the Cessna dipped and bumped, Sienna tightened her hands around the seat rests.

"Afraid of flying?"

"No, not on bigger airplanes. This one on the other hand makes me extremely nervous."

"Don't worry. It won't take us long to get there."

Sienna watched the land grow smaller as they lifted up into the stark blue sky. Looking at the ground wasn't helping and looking at the instruments in front of her only made her edgy. She hated being thousands of feet in the air in a vehicle that she could neither understand nor control.

"Is Sandoval going to have your butt for this?"

"Hopefully, he'll just chew on it for a while."

"Why are you doing this?"

"I don't know…could it be that I care what happens to your brother?"

He gave her a disbelieving look. "All right. I put myself in your place and I couldn't turn my back on you, okay!" God, was she going soft in the head as well as the heart over this man? "Besides, I couldn't let you go alone. We're in this together," she groused.

The engines buzzed in her ears. "Why would he go all the way to Tahoe to sell the guns?" she asked.

"I think David's desperate to unload those weapons." A.J.'s mouth tightened as they left San Diego behind.

"And a desperate man makes mistakes?"

He shrugged. "Usually."

There was snow on the peaks to the north, and there were broad, flat valleys between the ridges. They were cruising low enough that she could make out cars along the highway, communities that were little huddles of houses, and the deep, thick green of the forest to the west.

Sienna tried to relax. "I'm sorry about what this is going to do to your family."

"It's going to kill my dad."

"He must have been so proud of your brother. It said in his jacket that he received the Congressional Medal of Honor for saving all those people in Angola."

"I still can't believe this." A.J's voice cracked and he kept his eyes straight ahead.

She reached out, her heart aching for him. Touching his tense forearm, she squeezed, feeling some of the tension release in him. "I know. It must seem so surreal to you."

After a moment of silence, she said. "I noticed that you call your stepfather Dad."

"Yeah."

"Why?"

"What do you mean, why? He's my dad."

"Not technically."

"You mean biologically?"

"Yes."

"There's more to being a father than genetic material. I call him Dad because he was there for me and he never wavered, not even through the nasty teenage years. He gave me discipline, morals and a backhand or two when I needed it."

"I call my foster father by his given name."

"Why?"

"My first foster father I called Dad, and the second. I guess by the time I got to Scott, I just thought, what was the point?"

"Was he there for you?"

"Yes. All the time."

"Sienna, 99.9 percent of being a father is showing up."

His words struck home and Sienna realized how true they were. All of them, Lynne, Scott and Michelle, had always stood by her through thick and thin. A memory came to her, one that she had buried. The day she had told them she would enter the police academy was one of the hardest days of her life. They hadn't wanted her to. They were worried about her safety, but in the end, they had never belittled her choice. Her whole family had shown up for her graduation, beaming with pride.

The sky, which had lookcd blue-gray when they had taken off, got grayer as they flew toward Nevada. The mountains loomed in the distance and Sienna wiped her slick hands on her slacks. She really didn't like small planes.

The plane dipped and the sky got darker and looked heavy with snow.

The silence stretched out between them and after a few hours in the air, the fear she'd been holding inside dug at her like rending claws. One minute they were flying through a leaden sky, the next it was as if a white blanket had dropped over them. Ice pelted the windshield of the small plane and Sienna reached for A.J.'s arm.

"This looks bad."

A.J. nodded his head. "It sure does. We're not far from Tahoe," he said through gritted teeth.

While she tried to calm her fears, A.J. got on the radio and let the Tahoe airport know that he was coming in for a landing. He banked the plane and headed toward the airport.

The ice storm continued to batter the plane and Sienna held on until they could see the blinking lights of a runway. Sienna turned to tell A.J., but he'd already seen them and was guiding the plane toward them.

She watched him take on the storm; his calm eyes and easy movements reassured her. The sure way he flew made something in her change. Her stomach dropped, but it had nothing to do with their slow descent. He made her feel safe and with a wonder that grew and moved through her like a tidal wave, she realized that she trusted him. Trusted him to land the plane with the same calm he used while flying it.

A strong wind buffeted the plane, the frigid air reaching her in the cockpit. A.J.'s hands were steady on the controls. She could see the sheet of ice that was the runway, realizing that the crew was having a hard time keeping up with the frigid conditions. They'd made it to this airfield just in time. Even fifteen minutes later might have spelled disaster. She held her breath as the small wheels contacted with the salted asphalt and fought for purchase. A.J. braked the plane and it skidded from side to side as he diminished the speed until they stopped.

He turned to her, his eyes still the same steady electric blue. "Piece of cake," he said.

Sienna laughed, surprised at her response. The man was incorrigible.

"Laughter in the face of danger. A woman after my own heart."

"I'm not after your heart."

"What if it's already yours?"

For a moment Sienna stilled even as A.J. looked down and undid his seat belt. She saw the flush of red across his cheekbones. The embarrassment on his face caused her heart to leap in her chest.

"A.J."

"Right, I know, not the time nor the place."

It was painful to realize that she was half in love with him. Painful because she saw no future in a relationship with a SEAL. He would be gone too long to places unknown and into terrible danger. And she could lose him as quickly as she found him. Lose him like she lost her parents and all the other foster families that came after them. It would be like being in love with a ghost. No. There would be no safety in that. It wasn't for her. She undid her belt and pushed open the door of the plane.

Men were already there in heavy winter clothing, putting chocks under the wheels of the plane and escorting them to the small terminal.

"You just barely made it," a man shouted over the howl of the cold wind. "We were just about to close."

"How long do you think this will last?" Sienna shouted back.

"No way to know. Most likely overnight. Freak ice storms in the mountains are not uncommon this time of year. Bottom line is you're not going anywhere tonight, lady."

Sienna stopped walking, the howling wind clutching at her hair and whipping it around her chilled face.

A.J. bumped into her and with the warmth of his body propelled her into the terminal.

She rounded on him. "Did you hear that?"

"What?"

"We could be stuck here maybe into tomorrow."

"I know," he said grimly.

Just then a terminal employee approached them and Sienna had to stop the flow of anxious words that wanted to spew from her lips. She bit her tongue as A.J. negotiated for lodgings. They were able to get a cabin at a nearby ski resort.

Sienna tried to use her cell phone in the airport to call Captain Sandoval, but she couldn't get through. A Good Samaritan employee with a four-wheel drive drove them the three miles to the resort. The roads were treacherous and they almost skidded off the road three times.

The guy got them settled, turning on the heat and electricity. Sienna used the phone in the lobby to call her Captain and he hollered at her for fifteen minutes before ordering her to give him updates.

The small cabin was sumptuous with a huge field-stone fireplace, a large sunken tub and a loft bedroom.

Once inside, Sienna noticed that A.J. was watching until the guy drove off. He put his hand on the knob.

"Where are you going?"

"There's a four-wheel drive parked out front."

"Are you suggesting we steal a car?"

"We're not going to steal it. We're just going to borrow it."

"That's splitting hairs."

He whirled on her. "Do you think I give a damn about the law right now? I've got to find my brother."

He twisted the knob and pulled the door open.

Refusing to give in, she slammed her hand against the door and braced her feet. "A.J., running off into the night isn't going to help David."

"I can't lose him, Sienna."

"I know. But you've got to give me time to find him. It's too dangerous to go out there now. We could end up wrapped around a tree. Who will help David then?"

He abandoned the door and paced into the foyer. "Don't make me hurt you."

"Give it your best shot, buster."

He closed his eyes and leaned his head back. "You are the biggest pain in the ass."

"Takes one to know one."

"I'm only going to ask one more time."

She rushed him. As she struck him, her momentum took them into the living room, over the couch and onto the living room floor.

A.J. landed on his back with a thud, Sienna sprawled on top of him.

She felt him give in. "You knew I wouldn't hurt you," he admitted.

"You'll never bluff me."

She pushed herself up on her elbows to look into his face. When she did her heart twisted. His eyes had a sheen to them, his face contorting.

Sienna reacted, whispering, "It'll be okay." She caught him by the back of the neck, the frustration and need inside her overflowing. She didn't know what to do with it. The emotions inside her made her frantic to comfort him. The hot skin of his neck seemed to sear her until she was gasping. The tension between them was always high, but here in this isolated place, Sienna felt out of her element. Before she realized what she was about to do, her mouth was on his with a frenzy. The hot moist feel of his lips made her only hunger for more as she literally began to rip at his coat, her nails sliding against the leather with a tearing sound.

After his first startled gasp, he moaned into her mouth, bringing his body flush with hers.

She felt as if she were unraveling, a sensation that only he could invoke. It made her grapple with his clothes in an attempt to get to the smooth, hot muscle beneath. His calm, his sheer tenacity while flying the plane rocketed through her brain and only made her want to get closer to him. He was the only man she cared about in all her adult life. She wanted his brother to be safe, but more importantly, she wanted A.J. to be safe. There was no way she'd let him run out into the ice storm to find David.

She was weak where he was concerned and she

knew it. She couldn't fight it. She'd turned her back on Captain Sandoval and her cop family and run after him.

He made her insides jangle.

She was out of control

She was wild.

She loved it.

She reached down and palmed the ridge of flesh straining against the fly of his jeans.

His response was instantaneous. His hand slipped around the back of her neck as he pulled her down to his mouth. "Sienna," he said just before he captured her lips.

She murmured as he broke away from her. "Let me help. Stay with me. We'll find him. I promise."

What she felt right now was beyond her imagination. She should have run from this passion. It was consuming her, but she couldn't seem to care. The heat of him against her skin was like a potent aphrodisiac; the musky male scent of him made her head swim, her heart triple beat. She pressed her hands to the soft cotton and it wasn't enough. It wasn't satisfying; it made her more frantic. Only his naked skin could satisfy her. She yanked on his T-shirt and A.J. said, "Sienna, you're strangling me."

She pulled harder. "Get it off."

A.J. rose, grabbed at her hands. Softly, he whispered, "Slow down, babe. Slow down. This is not going to happen on the floor, or the couch. I want you in a bed.''

"A.J." was all she managed to say as she pressed her body against his. He made a soft, deeply satisfied sound in the back of his throat that made Sienna crazy.

They moved in tandem as he backed her down the hall, simultaneously battling with her attempt to remove his shirt and propel her where he wanted her to go.

"Dammit, Sienna…" he gasped as she palmed him hard.

She felt as if she'd waited a lifetime to feel this way and it was overwhelming her. She had to have him naked, hot and out of control beneath her hands. She pressed him against the wall.

The longing pulled at her like a fast-moving current. As if there weren't enough minutes in her life to get enough of him.

He tried to remove her hand, but she'd already gotten his fly unzipped, his jeans were already halfway around his hips. She reached down and slipped her hand inside his underwear, taking what she wanted. He was exquisitely hard, exquisitely male.

He shuddered and groaned, pressing up into her palm in an uncontrollable, undulating movement of his hips.

He grabbed her wrist, breathing hard. "Sienna. If you keep this up, it's going to end before it begins."

She let go of him in one long caress, and he jerked against her hand.

She grabbed his T-shirt and pulled it over his head. She heard him laugh, but the sound got strangled in his throat when she pulled off her shirt. He drank in the sight of her, making Sienna feel like the most desirable woman on the planet.

He closed his eyes, pressing his forehead to hers.

''Damn you, you make me crazy,'' she whispered, her mouth going to the heated steel muscles she bared. Pressing her lips to his salty, musky flesh, she kissed the exposed skin of his enticing flesh, trailing her fingertips along hard muscle.

He moaned softly on an indrawn breath. When her tongue came out and licked his flat nipple, she swallowed as excitement coursed through her. She couldn't help doing it again, this time gently sucking the hard nub.

Breathing hard, his whole body jerked, his head falling back, his eyes closing in sensual rapture.

In a quick, deft movement he picked her up around the waist and headed for the closest bed. Sienna struggled. She wanted, wanted, wanted until she couldn't think, breathe or wait. He made it there just before she slipped out of his grasp.

She grabbed for him again. ''Wait.''

But she couldn't. A.J. captured her hands and spun her around. He held her imprisoned against his chest. He took a long, shuddering breath.

With one hand he held on to her, with the other he unsnapped her jeans and worked them and her panties down her legs. He picked her up, kicked the jeans and panties away. His hand grabbed her naked hip and pulled her buttocks tight against his groin. Sienna moaned softly, unable to think straight. "Please, A.J., please," she pleaded.

"Ah, babe. You are so beautiful." He buried his face in her hair, thrusting his erection against her. He slid his hand down between her legs, stroking her where she so desperately needed to be touched. He let go of her wrists, and she arched her back, twining her arms around his neck. He slid his hand up her taut rib cage and cupped her full breast, his thumb stroking across her hard nipple. She cried out and bucked in his arms.

"Sienna," he whispered hoarsely as he moved with her toward the bed. He pushed her down, and followed her, but was up again, racing out of the room. When he came back he fumbled with the foil packet, while Sienna clutched at him. Her hands were at his waist, removing his jeans and underwear. The heat of him, the thickness of his muscles, and the heavy sound of his breathing made the need tighten within her again.

With quick movements, he protected her, then he was on her, shoving into her with his hands at her hips, pulling her toward him, breathing hard and raggedly and saying her name over and over.

She put her arms around his neck. His kiss was wide-open against her mouth as his body drove into her. The sensation engulfed her: the force of him, his hands pressed into her buttocks, pulling her up into him in his own impassioned cadence.

She wanted to cry out; she couldn't seem to breathe deeply enough for the sensation that dilated and spread inside her. She pressed upward and he drove into her, harder and harder, his thrusts pulling something impossible from within her, something crazy and frightening that she could not defend against.

He gripped her to him. She heard him making low sounds as if words were throttled in his chest. A deep tremor passed through him and into her, a powerful instant of suspension, with his face pressing into the curve of her shoulder.

Then, with a harsh rush of air between his teeth, he relaxed. He rested his forehead against her breast, breathing deeply, pulling back a little to put weight on his hands.

She felt him trembling with the awkwardness of the position, and it dawned on her with a shaky, hysterical little spurt of humor that he still had one foot on the floor.

"I'm glad you find this so funny. I've never been in such a precarious position while making love. You're a dangerous woman."

She laughed again. She couldn't seem to help it.

She felt as light as air. A.J. laughed, too, pushed up and away from her and stood.

He tilted his head, gave her a wry, bemused smile and went into the bathroom. She heard the water come on as if it was filling a basin.

He reached out his hand, and Sienna rose into his embrace. The feeling of his hard-muscled body naked against hers was luxurious.

He carried her into the bathroom to the sunken tub and immersed her in the water. Climbing in with her he proceeded to soap her, his hands running over every curve of her.

Soon, they were both panting from the sensual play and A.J. pushed her back and began to descend. Sienna caught his head. "What are you doing?"

"Going down."

"Under the water?"

"At BUD/S they had a nickname for me, too."

"What was that?"

"Shamu. I can hold my breath for a long time."

"You can."

"A very long time."

When his head descended and she felt the unique touch of his mouth intimately against her, she closed her eyes and let the world fade away.

LATER, THEY SAT together on one of the two sofas in the cavernous living room, the glow of the fireplace reflecting off the polished mahogany beams of the ceiling.

"Thanks for stopping me. You were right. It would have been a waste of resources and energy."

The quiet way he spoke set off sensations in her midriff that made her pulse skip and falter. He held her gaze, a bleak look in his eyes, and then he gently reached out and grabbed a thick strand of her hair, absently rubbing it between his fingers. He tugged gently.

"I've never cracked under battle conditions. It seems I get calmer. But today…"

"Was different. David's not a guy you serve with. He's your brother. The normal rules don't apply."

"I feel that somehow I've let him down. I've been gone so much and so long that I wonder if he needed me and I wasn't there."

"A.J., beating yourself up isn't going to help."

"Gibson told me that David needed the money. He had large gambling debts. Why didn't he go to my father?"

"Maybe he was too ashamed?"

"Maybe."

"Are you going to let your parents know what's going on?"

"No, this is not the kind of information you tell them over the phone."

"How long have your parents been married?"

"Twenty years. My mother worked for his campaign when he was a delegate. It was true love at first sight.''

''What happened to your father?''

''He was a merchant marine. I guess the ocean is in my blood. He split when I was a baby. Then it was just my mom and I.''

''How old were you when they married?''

''Six. It was tough for my mom, barely making ends meet. My mom worked two jobs, but I never went hungry or felt neglected.''

He paused and looked at her with those arresting eyes. ''I was seven when David was born. He was...a great baby. Smart kid. Used to follow me around all the time. Followed me right into the military.''

She wrapped her arms around him.

''I don't know what happened to change him.''

''Life has a way of changing people,'' she said, holding him tight.

It was late when they finally went to bed. Drawing the covers over her, A.J. walked to the light switch, giving Sienna a stirring view of his taut buttocks.

''I've been meaning to tell you this. You have a very nice ass, Camacho.''

He chuckled in the darkness. When he slipped into bed, she immediately curled against him with a sigh.

There would be the future to face, but here in the cocoon of his safe arms, it was as if her mind had separated from her body, and she didn't think further than physical awareness, the sensual heat of his embrace.

Her dreams were enough for this night.

SIENNA OPENED her eyes and the first thing she saw was A.J. moving in slow motion in a beautiful dance. The morning sun slanted across the floor, falling on his skin, turning it a golden hue. His dark hair glistened. Every time he moved, his muscles flexed in a rhythmic flow, a slow dance of spiraling movement that she couldn't look away from.

He kept his eyes focused straight ahead, didn't even glance at her, but she knew he was aware of her. She raised herself onto her elbow to watch the fluid athletic motion of his powerful body. A light sheen of sweat lay like a fine mist on his supple skin. She watched in fascinated interest as his muscles flexed and stretched in a pliant, superbly masterful way. His balance and undulating arms and legs worked in perfect unison and she was beginning to believe that self-defense and the resulting violence that came from these movements were only a small part of the overall meaning.

When his crystal blue eyes met hers, he smiled, coming to a position where his hands were together in front of him as if in prayer. Very slowly he bowed.

"What are you doing?" she asked, her voice husky.

"Trying to keep from coming out of my skin. Distract me some more. Come over here and I'll show you how it's done.''

"That was quite beautiful."

"I've been called a few names, but beautiful was never one of them."

She laughed. "I bet."

Sienna slipped out of bed and went to reach for her gown.

"You don't need that. Come over here."

She picked up one of their discarded towels from the night before and walked to him; his eyes were intent upon her face and she smiled.

She perceived a change in him, he seemed calmer, and more relaxed and she breathed a silent sigh of relief.

"I want you to promise me something," he said. She trailed the towel down from his neck to his shoulders and wiped off the perspiration that had accumulated down his torso.

"What?" she asked warily. "I don't usually make blind promises."

He tilted his head to study her. She traced her finger over one of the shrapnel scars, starting at the top of his shoulder and slashing down over his biceps. The feel of his taut, moist skin sent a shuddering warm sensation throughout her body. Her eyes finally met his.

"It's regarding David."

Her eyes fell and she bit her bottom lip, running

her delectable pink tongue over her dry lips. "A.J., don't ask me something that will make me choose between what I know is right and wrong."

He closed his eyes briefly. She held the towel against her like a shield; against what, she wasn't sure.

"All I'm saying is that I want to take the lead."

"You think he'll do something drastic?" She swallowed and stepped closer to him, mesmerized by the tender, pleading light she saw in his eyes. She put her hands on his damp shoulders, straining toward him, aching for him.

His hand came up and brushed strands of burnished hair off her cheek. "I'm just asking for you to relinquish that formidable control and let me handle it."

"All right."

He gave her a slow bright smile and she sighed and leaned against him. She realized how close she had gotten to him and it had nothing to do with the physical at all. She longed to tell him how she felt, but knew in the long run it didn't make any difference. She wasn't yet sure that she could even verbalize what she felt for him and the emotions were beginning to frighten her.

"So, do you have any other deadly moves you can teach me?"

"Tae Kwon Do isn't about violence, Sienna. It's about centering yourself. Becoming aware of yourself enables you to use positive energy and understand that thoughts motivate intentions.''

He turned her so that her bare back was against his damp chest. ''The original intention of the art was aimed at the development of individuality by steadfast courage in fighting for the cause of justice and peace, even in a life-and-death situation. And above all it is aimed at developing knowledge of the importance of total devotion to a spirit of humanity and achievement of self-discipline in mind and body.''

''So you're saying that it is more than a way of violent fighting. It's a way to meld the mind and the body to achieve peace with oneself and others?''

''You're very perceptive, Sienna.''

''So, have you achieved self-perfection?''

''Hardly. We say we are always learning, always experiencing what life has to offer. Only when we strive to achieve such elements as courage, fortitude, dedication, loyalty and—importantly—honor can we know and master ourselves.''

She listened to his soft calm voice and knew he had achieved all those virtues and more. Recalled the way he had tried not to take advantage of her in a weak moment, the way he held her, the worry over his brother and the way he had backed her up. She knew that he lived these teachings and that those virtues were woven into the very fabric of his soul. It was thrilling to find another layer of A.J., one more fascinating piece of the puzzle.

She turned and touched his face lightly. "You possess all of those, especially honor."

The words seemed to curl around him like smoke. They soaked into his skin becoming the blood that ran through his veins. He cupped her face, his thumbs caressing her delicate cheekbones. Her wide eyes connected with his and he felt a wrenching deep inside him as if somehow they joined and became one for a brief breathless heart-aching moment.

He knew she felt it, too, by the emotion he saw in her eyes. She stared at him in awe and amazed wonder.

He covered her mouth with his in a gentle, tender kiss using his willpower to hold the dark need rising in him. He perceived that she was still afraid of her emotions, still afraid of what he did to her.

She clung to him, offering her lips up to his like a sacrifice. His body ached and throbbed with desire, pushing at his rigid control, threatening to snap it like a dry brittle stick.

Instead, he began to move using his arms, torso and legs to bring Sienna with him. Their naked bodies absorbed the sheen of labor and the glow of desire.

When she came to the final position, he slipped his hands around her waist and drew her toward him. His skin was hot against hers, his hands sliding up her rib cage to cup her breasts, a gentle, warm caress that made her groan softly against his kneading fingers.

"I love that sound, Sienna."

He lowered his head as he swept his lips across the place where her shoulder met her neck.

The phone by the bedside table jangled and she quickly separated from him. Sienna walked over to the phone and picked it up. She listened for a few beats, grabbed a piece of paper and scribbled down an address.

When she put down the receiver, she walked back to him. "Captain Sandoval said that David just used his credit card to rent a cabin. I've got the address."

ONCE AT THE CABIN, they used quick movements and stealth to get to the front porch. Sienna looked quickly into the window and what she saw made her blood run cold.

A man lay on the floor, his arms flung wide, and a gun next to his outstretched fingers.

She turned to look at A.J. and his face contorted in pain. For a moment he bowed his head. When his head lifted his eyes were cold and empty.

Without warning, he kicked the door open and went in. Two men came out of nowhere and tackled him to the floor.

As Sienna came through the door a man went for her gun. He backhanded her across the face, making her see stars. Balling up her fist, she hit him a stunning blow to the jaw and he released her gun.

Sienna had only a moment to sight down the barrel before she was grabbed around the neck and a gun was shoved into her back.

"Drop it," the steely voice said.

12

SIENNA DIDN'T immediately obey. She recognized that voice.

"Agent Norton."

"Detective Parker?"

"I thought you weren't involved in tracking down David Buckner. Somebody at the NIS is going to hear about this."

"What the hell is going on?" A.J.'s voice snapped out, sounding as crisp as the cold morning air.

"And Lieutenant Camacho," Norton said. An agent scooped up her gun and Norton released her.

Sienna reached out her hand to help A.J. up.

A.J. shook off the help of a man who came close to him. He shoved another man out of the way to get to the body.

In the corner, handcuffed to a heavy wooden chair, another man sat with a sullen and terrified look in his eyes.

"What's going on?"

"The body is Ray Merchant. Don't worry. He'll live and the man in the corner is—"

"Tyrone Knight," Sienna said.

She felt such relief that it wasn't David who lay on the floor.

A.J. knelt near the body, his face ashen. With a growl, he launched himself at Agent Norton.

It took three men to get him off.

"Let him go. He has a right to be angry." Agent Norton put up his hand to ward off the other agents and they let go of A.J.

"They tracked my brother's credit card. You used it to get them here."

"Yes."

"Where is my brother?" A.J. demanded.

"Somewhere safe. He's working for us."

THEY WERE IN the living room of the cabin. Under heavy guard, Ray Merchant had been taken to the nearest hospital for medical attention and Tyrone was being transferred to the local police jail for safekeeping.

A fire blazed in the fireplace and Sienna leaned back into the couch, soaking up the heat.

"I'm sorry, Detective Parker," Rob Norton said as he handed her an ice pack to put on her eye. "We'd just taken down Knight and Merchant. We thought you were the second wave."

Sienna gave the man a scowling look as she placed the cooling bag against her sore eye and jaw. "How about you give us an explanation to make amends."

"First of all, I'm not with NIS."

"Who are you with?" Sienna asked, wincing when her jaw moved. "Wait a minute. Don't tell me. Let me guess. The FBI."

"Right.

"You're after Jack Taylor?"

"Not exactly."

"Who, then?"

"Jimmy Lee Moran."

"Who is that?"

"He's the head of a militia group called Freedom Fighters of the New Revolution."

"So Jack Taylor was your conduit to Moran?"

"I'm afraid so."

"Why my brother?" A.J. growled. She could still see the anger simmering in his eyes.

"He's smart and thinks quick on his feet. We needed someone undercover who worked at the base to hook up with Merchant. After looking at your brother's jacket, there wasn't any question he could handle the job."

"How does Merchant fit into this?" Sienna asked, rubbing at her jaw.

"He's the naval base weapons manager and Jack Taylor's flunky."

"He was stealing the weapons for Jack?" Sienna said.

"How did it work?" A.J. asked.

"We asked David to get word around that he had money troubles. We even had him gamble and lose to set up his cover. He started to talk about how he'd do anything to earn a few extra bucks. It wasn't long before Merchant contacted him and offered him the job of driving for Taylor. He liked that David was security.''

"So the FBI was onto the theft."

"Yeah. We had Merchant and Taylor cold, but we weren't after them. We needed David to find out how to contact Moran. He did so through Knight."

"Knight was double-crossing Taylor?"

"Right."

"What was Knight doing in Rojas's operation?"

"He was Taylor's inside man. Taylor always liked to know what his competition was up to. Knight met David and told him if he needed quick cash to get out of the country, sell to Moran. Knight said he would give David the information for a cut of the gun money."

"You told the D.A. to back off on Knight. Why? David already had the information about Moran."

"We couldn't afford to spook Taylor by having Rojas implicate him through Knight. We needed Taylor in play."

"And now you have Knight to make a case against Taylor," A.J. said. "Nice and neat. Two birds with one stone."

"You were holding up my serial number and fingerprints so that I couldn't confirm that David was involved," Sienna confirmed.

"Correct. David was under deep cover. We couldn't take the chance that anything about this operation would be leaked. Keeping you in the dark was the only way to protect him."

"A little professional courtesy would have gone a long way."

"We didn't expect your quick and top-notch detective work. When you found the truck and collared Rojas with that airtight case, we knew that it wouldn't be long before you ended up heading over to the base. We're glad Rojas is out of business. He was our next target." Norton smiled at her, and said, "You interested in working for the FBI?"

"If you hire her, Norton, you better watch your job," A.J. said.

"Now, I'm going to have to ask you two to stay put. We're going to rendezvous with Moran."

A.J. jumped up, his fists clenched. "If you think I'm sitting here and waiting while my brother goes into danger, you're crazy."

"Look Camacho. I'll bring your brother back here when we're though, but I can't have him distracted by you. You stay."

A.J. PACED like a caged panther, all grace and power. Every so often he'd stop and look out the window.

She left him alone, knowing that there was nothing she could say or do that would alleviate his anxiety. They were both playing a waiting game.

Sienna looked down at her watch and her stomach lurched. It was six o'clock and her sister's wedding rehearsal was over and the dinner was just beginning. She closed her eyes and leaned her head back wearily.

She should have called, but she remembered her sister's words. *Don't bother to get fitted. Don't bother to come at all.*

"What's wrong?" A.J. asked, sitting down next to her.

"I'm missing the rehearsal dinner. The wedding is tomorrow and I don't even have my gown ready. I'm afraid she'll never forgive me."

"She's your sister. She'll forgive…"

"It's not your fault. We thought David's life was in danger. I don't regret the choice I made."

He pulled her against him, holding her, comforting her the way she'd comforted him yesterday.

Exhaustion and the warmth of the fire lulled Sienna to sleep. The next thing she knew, she heard the door to the cabin open.

A.J. felt intense relief to see David standing in the doorway, his right arm in a sling, looking like he could conquer the world.

"A.J.!"

"David!"

The two brothers met and hugged tightly.

"Damn, I'm glad to see you," A.J. said.

David hugged him back with one arm, a catch in his voice. "Me, too, A.J. Me, too."

"What happened to your arm?"

"I twisted my shoulder taking down Moran."

Sienna came over and extended her hand. "Hi, David. It's nice to finally meet you. We've been looking for you."

David shook Sienna's hand with his left. "I know. Norton filled me in. I'm really sorry. I couldn't contact anyone, I couldn't risk it."

Sienna moved away to give him some privacy with his brother. A.J. turned to David. "So, my brother the undercover operative."

"I know you were worried about me, but I have to tell you, it's been great. I'm sorry I twisted my shoulder. I won't get to see the look on Jack's face when they take him down."

David glanced over at Sienna who was talking to Rob.

David's sharp brown eyes studied A.J., taking in every detail. "So what's with the cop?"

"What do you mean?"

"Come on. I've already seen the way she looks at you."

"What way?"

"Like you're water and she's really thirsty."

"We're hanging out."

"Jeez, brother, you don't even know how bad you have it," David said.

Rob Norton was having a heated discussion

with Sienna. Finally the man broke off and approached them.

"It's time to go after Taylor, but David can't drive or handle a weapon."

A.J. looked at Sienna, who was frowning at him, then he looked at David. "I'll drive in David's place."

"Let's give them his guns, then."

"Damn right," A.J. said.

"TAYLOR."

"This is David Buckner," A.J. said. They had landed just thirty minutes ago and had immediately gone to Captain Sandoval's office to get organized.

"Where are my weapons?" Taylor demanded.

"Not so fast." A.J. shifted the phone in his hand. "It seems that my hope to sell the guns to Moran didn't work out. The FBI shut him down. Next they'll be coming after me and if they do, I'm not going down alone. I need cash and I need it fast."

"Tell me where and when."

A.J. looked at his watch. It was eight o'clock. "Twenty-Ninth Street pier in one hour."

"I SHOULD BE the one to drive the truck," A.J. said for the third time.

"I don't like it," Sienna insisted.

"I want a piece of this action. They've threatened my brother."

"I'm inclined to allow him to do this," Agent Norton said. "We jerked you around about your brother. If you want in, you've got it."

"But..."

"Do you doubt his ability?" Norton asked.

"No," Sienna said, trying to keep her voice down. Her heart was lodged in her throat. She knew she was being irrational about this. She knew it, but she couldn't help herself.

"Then why don't you want him to participate?"

"He's not a cop," she said stubbornly, unwilling to say what she really felt.

"He's a Navy SEAL, Detective Parker."

"They'll be gunning for the person in the truck, Norton and you know it. He's a sitting target."

"Camacho?"

"I've been in situations a lot worse than this, Norton. I can handle it and you owe me."

"If you go, I go. I'm going to be right beside you under the dash on the passenger's side."

"No," A.J. barked.

"What is with you two?" Norton looked from A.J. to Sienna and back again. "How did you ever agree on anything in this investigation? Camacho, you drive the truck. Parker, you cover him. Discussion over. Let's suit up. There will be a briefing in thirty minutes."

Sienna walked out of the captain's office still not

happy about Norton's decision, but at least she'd be A.J.'s back up.

When they reached the tactical room to pick up their vests, A.J. grabbed her by the arm and pulled her into an empty room.

"Is this about the grenade injury? Don't think I can pull my own weight?"

"No. It's not about that and I would never hold that against you."

"Then why?"

"You're not a cop!" she said, feeling the passion, the love, and the fear well up inside her.

"I've logged an enormous amount of mission time. I've led operations. I've gone into hostile environments and rescued hostages and took shrapnel. What is it about your stringent rules and regulations that you just can't let go of? Do you have to control everything?"

"This isn't about control," she shouted.

"What's it about then?" he yelled back.

"I don't want you to get hurt," she cried.

For a moment A.J. just stared at her, then he grabbed her and pulled her against him, his mouth consuming hers in a wild kiss that left her breathless.

"I don't want you to get hurt, either, but we're both professionals. We can handle it."

"Just don't do anything stupid or heroic."

There was a knock on the door and Norton stuck

his head in. "If you two are finished yelling at each other, could you please join us?"

THE NIGHT WAS pitch-black with barely any moon. Under the dash in the truck, Sienna could hardly see a thing.

"We're almost there."

"Good, I'm getting a cramp."

"Lady, you've been a cramp in my butt from day one."

"Shut up."

"Not good," A.J. said softly.

"What?"

"Two of the streetlights are off."

"That should work to our advantage. Taylor won't realize you're not David until it's too late."

The truck ground to a halt and A.J. put the vehicle in park and shut off the engine. They waited in the darkness. Two bright headlights cut across the gloom and illuminated A.J.'s face for just a moment. Sienna drank in the sight of him, vowing that she wouldn't let him down.

"Show time," A.J. whispered as headlights flashed over the truck.

"Are they armed?" Sienna asked, her stomach fluttering.

"Don't see any weapons, but they have coats on."

"How many?"

"Five. Two by the vehicle and three on their way here."

The three men came up to the truck and A.J. rolled the window down a fraction. "Do you have the money?" he asked.

Taylor swore and held up the briefcase for A.J. to see.

"Pass it to me through the window."

A.J. took the case and set it in the seat beside him, never taking his eyes off Taylor or the other two men just behind him.

The passenger side door was jerked open. A man with a gun stood silhouetted against the moon. Sienna kicked out and the man grunted as the gun discharged. She was up and out from under the dashboard, hitting the man's nose with the heel of her hand. She heard glass shatter as he went down in a heap. Racing around to the other side of the truck, she was faced with another of Taylor's flunkies. With quick and efficient movements she brought him down, too.

The two by the car had already jumped in and sped toward the exit only to be blocked by the FBI cars pouring onto the scene.

A.J. was still seated, struggling with a man who'd shoved a gun through the broken window.

The gun went off in a series of loud blasts. As the hammer clicked against an empty chamber, A.J. opened the door and knocked the man to the ground where Sienna held him immobile with her gun.

A.J.'s head whipped around looking for Taylor.

"Don't do it. Wait for backup," she ordered.

"Sorry, Sienna, but he's mine," he said.

A.J. took off and Sienna's eyes followed him. Taylor was heading for a boat at a nearby pier.

Sienna called out to A.J., but he didn't heed her. She felt as if her heart was being split in two. The thought of losing him cut her so deep, she gasped.

The FBI agents arrived and as soon as an agent took over for her, Sienna headed after A.J.

Sienna spotted A.J. as he reached the end of the pier. Taylor stopped, a gun materializing in his hand. A.J. never slowed and his momentum took them both off the pier into the water below.

When she reached the edge of the pier, they were nowhere to be found. She lived a lifetime in those few moments, knowing that loving him would kill her, knowing that the thought of him in danger every day would be too much for her to endure.

Finally he surfaced, and relief flashed through her. Although he was safe, Sienna knew that he had been hers to take, but he could never be hers to hold.

THE NEXT FEW HOURS was filled with paperwork and booking the perpetrators, talking to the FBI.

Finally they were free to leave.

"Come to my apartment, Sienna. I want to make love to you all night on the beach."

"I can't."

"Later?"

"I don't think so."

"What are you saying?"

"All this time you've been bucking procedure and doing what you want. Taking risks. It wouldn't work between us, A.J. Just leave it at that."

"I'm not leaving it like that. I love you. Don't you get it? Nothing means more to me now than you do."

The look on his face broke her heart, but the emotions inside her were too overwhelming, swamping her like a tidal wave. She felt as if she were drowning in them. "I can't be with a man who risks too much."

"And you don't risk anything at all," he said quietly.

"What are you talking about?" The little jeering voice inside her became a shout, telling her that he was right.

"When it comes to your heart. You hide behind your job and all the varied reasons we can't be together. It's all crap. You're trying to keep yourself safe from the feelings inside you. But it doesn't make you safe, Sienna. It makes you alone. You cut yourself off from the people you care about."

"I do not. My job is demanding and there are a lot of reasons…"

"When you can stop lying to yourself, maybe then you'll see the truth."

He turned and walked away, but then stopped and came back. "I almost forgot. Here's your souvenir." And he pinned his trident SEAL insignia to the lapel of her jacket.

13

THIS IS IT. She'd gone too far. As she stood in the empty hall where the rehearsal dinner had been, she could almost hear the echo of laughter, almost feel the closeness, almost embrace the happiness.

She squeezed her eyes closed and realized in that instant how much her sister meant to her. How much she'd used her job, to not only keep everyone away, but isolate herself as well.

She had to let go of the past because Lynne, Scott and Michelle were not going to disappear from her life. She didn't have to protect herself from loving them too much.

She got in her car and drove until she found herself in front of Station House 82. She sat behind the wheel for a few minutes, and then got out.

"Hey, Detective Parker!" Sean O'Neill said, looking up from polishing the chrome of the front bumper of the big red engine.

Big, gorgeous, sandy-haired Sean with the wickedly seductive smile. Lana didn't have a chance, Sienna thought.

"Is Lana on duty?"

"She's on KP duty," Sean snickered.

"Thanks," Sienna said and as she passed him, she gave him a high five.

"Stay cool, baby," he said and went back to polishing the chrome.

When she entered the kitchen, Lana was wiping down the big table that accommodated the large crew.

"Sienna? Don't you have Michelle's dinner tonight."

Sienna bit her lip. "I had to handle the Buckner case."

Lana pulled out a chair. "Sit down. Are you okay?"

Sienna sank into the chair, running her hands through her hair. "Not really. I don't know how Michelle and my parents will ever forgive me."

"Sienna, they will understand. Just explain it to them."

"A.J. was right. I am using my job to keep myself safe from emotions. I've been afraid to show anything and it's irrational."

Lana sat down next to her. "You've been jerked around so much. It's understandable that you would feel this way. Go to them. Tell them. They'll understand."

"I should have realized that I was putting off the fittings and the dinners and using my job as a smoke screen. They're so wonderful."

"It's not too late."

Sienna wiped at the moisture on her cheeks. "You're right. It's not."

Lana walked with her to Sienna's car. There she hugged Lana. "Thank you. What would I do without you and Kate?"

"You don't have to do without us, ever."

She drove back to the division and went to her database. From her purse, she retrieved the card with the bridal shop owner's name on it. Using her power as a police officer, Sienna looked up the home address for the woman.

While she was driving over to the woman's house, her beeper went off. Using her cell phone, she dialed the number.

The voice on the other end of the line told her that they needed her at the division for an interrogation.

Firmly she said, "I'm off the clock. Someone else can handle it."

THE NEXT MORNING Sienna made her way to the church vestibule. She took a deep breath before twisting the knob. When she opened the door, Michelle, Lynne and Scott turned toward her. When they saw her, her mother burst into tears.

Scott came forward. "Don't mind her. She's been doing that all morning."

He put his arm around her and she was so grateful to him.

Michelle stood there waiting for Sienna and it was

all Sienna could do to take those few steps toward her sister.

"Are you still talking to me?" Sienna asked.

"Of course I'm still talking to you."

"I'm sorry." They both said in unison and a heavy weight lifted from Sienna's heart.

"Let me—"

"Tell me—"

"You go first," Sienna said.

"After that outburst in your office, I went back, but you had already left. Your captain told me what was going on. You should have told me a man's life was at stake. I know that your job is important to you."

Tears stung Sienna's eyes and she said very softly, "But I have to find a balance and I haven't. I have to confess to you that I wasn't even aware that I was using my job to keep emotional distance from you and Lynne and Scott. I was so afraid of loving you."

"Why?"

"It was so hard when I was shuffled from foster home to foster home that it was just easier to protect myself from getting attached. But I realized that I don't have to protect myself anymore from love. I don't want to lose you."

Michelle stepped forward and wrapped her arms around Sienna, and the tears flowed. "You could never lose our love. You're my big sister and I need you in my life. I want you to stand up with me while

I pledge myself to Geoff.'' Michelle looked down at Sienna's dress. "How did you get your dress altered so quickly?"

"I used DMV and a little pleading and begging. Thank God, the owner of the bridal shop is an understanding woman."

"And if she hadn't been?"

"I would have hated to have to threaten to throw her in jail."

Michelle smiled. "Would you help me dress?"

"Yes." Sienna accepted the exquisite wedding gown from her mother. "Thanks…Mom."

Her mother smiled with full acknowledgment in her eyes.

"If you're going to call her Mom, then I damn well better be Dad," her father said.

They all laughed. Her dad went off to see how things were going in the church. Sienna helped Michelle to pull the ivory lace dress up over her hips, smoothing the satin underskirt and bodice, and adjusting it so the slit in the straight skirt lay along her left leg ending at the knee.

Sienna pulled up the yards and yards of the shining satin train and attached it to the elegant satin bow at the small of Michelle's back while her mother worked at closing the numerous satin-covered buttons.

When those tasks were done, Sienna placed the pearl-and-sequin-decorated Juliet cap on her sister's head, pulling it forward until the peak settled comfortably against her forehead.

"I brought you something to wear."

She took the bracelet her sister had given her years ago off her wrist. The blue stones shone in the light. With a smile and tears welling in her eyes, Sienna slipped the friendship bracelet onto her sister's wrist. "Something borrowed, something blue."

A.J. LOOKED at his watch as he crouched in the reeds waiting for the helo to pick them up. Moments after he'd left Sienna, he'd been deployed. He wondered if she would ever be able to let go of the need to be safe.

He heard the blades of the Huey making the familiar *whop-whop* sound as it moved through the night. He grabbed the U.S. diplomat he'd just rescued from terrorists by the back of the jacket. "When I say go, we go."

The man nodded. As soon as the Huey landed, A.J. made the signal to head for the chopper. His team rose seemingly out of the ground and made their way to the waiting ride.

As the chopper lifted up into the air, A.J. let the rush of emotions regarding Sienna come to the fore. He intended to ask his commander for some R and R when he got back to base. It was all he could do to keep his concentration on the mission at hand. She was never far from his thoughts.

If only he could resist the memories that refused to diminish. But he wasn't able to resist her, he admitted. The sexual tension that crackled between them would have overwhelmed a stronger man than he. And the other things—her gentleness, her caring, her kindness—those things overwhelmed him even more. She had made him feel more alive than he had ever felt in his life.

He needed her. He needed Sienna in ways that had absolutely nothing to do with the incendiary sexual attraction he felt for her. And the thought of never holding her in his arms again opened up a chasm in his spirit, a place that would ever afterward be empty.

As a SEAL he knew about patience. It would be hard to wait for her to come to him. But she had to understand who she was and what was holding her back. Until then, no amount of talking to her would make a difference.

"WHAT ARE YOU doing here, David?"

"In all the confusion, I guess I never gave you an official statement. Someone called and said I had to come by the station house and see you."

"Sure. Have a seat. How are things going?"

"Pretty well. My shoulder is a lot better."

"That's great. How's your family?"

"Mom and Dad are fine. A.J. is leaving today on this top secret, hush-hush mission that's really dangerous. Of course, every time A.J. goes on a mission it's dangerous, but this one sounds really dangerous.''

Sienna jumped up from her chair. ''Hey, Robbie, could you take this guy's statement?'' she called. ''Where is A.J. now?''

''He's in Coronado, probably getting ready to deploy.''

''I need to see him.''

''Who's stopping you?''

SIENNA RUSHED OUT of the building and put on her siren as she drove to the base. When she got there, the guard walked over. She flashed her badge.

''Yes, Detective Parker, arrangements have been made for you.''

Sienna didn't bother to question her good luck. She drove onto the base, following the directions the guard at the gate had given her.

She got out of the car and saw two figures on the beach just coming out of the water.

''A.J.!'' she called and began running down the sandbank. A.J.'s head snapped up at the sound of her voice. He watched as she came flying across the sand, throwing herself into his arms. The smell of him, the warmth of his face against hers was like the same wonderful feeling of coming home.

''I was wrong about you, about us. Please tell me it's not too late. I love you.''

He closed his eyes, a shuddering breath easing out

of him. "It would never be too late." He cupped her face between his hands. "I still love you. I don't think I could live without you."

Her gaze softened and she smiled. "You were right. I was using my job to keep my family away emotionally. I was trying to do that to you with all my excuses as to why we couldn't be together. I don't want to be safe anymore. I want to take a risk on you."

His mouth was hot on hers. Her system overloaded, her pulse heavy, her heart laboring against it. She was so sure if he stopped kissing her, she would cease to exist. The sensation was like being absorbed into a heated vortex where she was lost and out of control, but she knew in A.J.'s arms she would always be anchored.

A.J. slid his fingers into her hair, cupping the side of her head as he deepened the kiss. Sienna made a helpless sound and opened her mouth. A.J.'s tongue slipped inside in a deep, searching kiss that drove every ounce of strength out of her body and made her knees buckle.

When he broke the kiss, she looked up into his hot blue eyes and knew that she and A.J. would make a wonderful life together. "Would you mind being married to a Navy SEAL instructor?"

"What?

"It's time for me to enter a different phase in my life. Even though I'm still in excellent shape, I'll never be where I was before that grenade. If I'm one second too late off the mark, it could spell disaster for a mission. This way I can contribute and still be part of the teams.''

''Not the instructor part, the married part. I don't care what you do, only that you love me.''

''That was a backhanded way of asking you to marry me.''

''The answer is still yes.''

''Then we're home free, Red.''

''Tell me something,'' she asked as they began to walk up the beach. ''You don't look like you're getting ready for a mission.''

''Who told you that?''

Sienna started to laugh.

''David,'' A.J. said. ''Family—you can't pick 'em....''

''And you can't live without them,'' Sienna said, looking up into his eyes.

Epilogue

SIENNA COULDN'T think of any place more comfortable to meet A.J.'s parents than the house she'd grown up in. She came through the front door, a bag of groceries in one arm and a bouquet of fresh flowers in the other.

The smell of roasted chicken hit her the closer she got to the kitchen. Cutting through the dining room, she smiled when she saw the table all decked out.

"Hi, sweetheart," her mother said, kissing her on the cheek and taking the bag from her. "Oh, the flowers are beautiful."

"I thought it'd be a nice touch. Thanks for putting on the fancy lace tablecloth."

"It's not every day that we meet the parents of the man our daughter is going to marry."

"Could it have had anything to do with the fact that A.J.'s father is a senator?"

"Mmm, maybe."

"Where's Dad?"

"Upstairs getting dressed. Call him. I think they just drove up."

Sienna went to the bottom of the stairs, but her father was already coming down.

"Hi there, sweetie. Got a kiss for your dad?"

"Sure do." She pressed a kiss to his cheek just as a knock sounded on the front door.

Her mother came in from the kitchen and they all opened the door. A.J. stood there with his mother and father.

"Come in," Sienna invited.

They stepped into the foyer. His mother was tall and willowy, of obvious Hispanic descent. His father had salt-and-pepper hair, the spitting image of David.

For a moment they all stood there in the silence until her father blurted out, "Want to see my new jigsaw?"

That broke the ice and every one laughed.

Her parents ushered A.J.'s parents into the living room. Sienna turned to A.J. and kissed his mouth.

Life was good. Taylor was behind bars awaiting trial while Jericho used Merchant and Knight to build an airtight case. Rojas was also going down and he'd implicated Knight in several murders. Tyrone Knight wouldn't be seeing the light of day anytime soon. David would be busy testifying against Jimmy Lee Moran in U.S. District Court, as well as acting as a witness for Jericho in his many prosecutions.

When she turned to go into the living room, he said, "Wait. You caught me off guard that day at the beach."

Her eyes fell to his hand and the velvet box he held. Holding it out to her, he said, "This is for you."

She took the box, but held her breath as she opened the lid and then it rushed out in admiration. The ring caught the light and flashed.

"I want everyone to know that you're mine."

He slipped the ring on her finger and Sienna wrapped her arms around him and held on.

"One more surprise. I put in my papers to become a SEAL instructor."

"You're sure this is what you want?"

"I'm sure. I promised to be honest with myself. Real courage was when you let your fears go and admitted to me that you loved me. Telling my commander that I couldn't continue as an active duty SEAL because of my injury was something I didn't want to face, but you gave me the courage to step up and be brave."

She cupped his face. "If it wasn't for you, I would never have realized what I was doing with my family and my fears."

"Looks like you took care of that. I want to make a life with you and I want to be here to do it. The best part is that I can still contribute to the SEALs."

"Life, love, happiness. Sounds pretty damn good to me. I'm glad I was a woman who dared and I have you and your trident pin to prove it."

"When do you get together with your friends again?"

"Not until we all have souvenirs."

"If we really tried," he whispered in her ear, "I bet we could come up with something much sexier than my trident pin."

"No. I don't think so, A.J. The pin is perfect. Just perfect."

Sienna wondered if her friends knew what they were getting themselves into. Lana, tough and determined and Kate, sweet and levelheaded. She hoped they learned as much from their journeys as Sienna had learned from hers.

"Sienna," her mother whispered from the hall. "Get in here quick before your father drags Senator Buckner into the garage."

"I don't know, Lynne," A.J. said with a wink to Sienna. "That's a damn fine jigsaw."

"Don't even joke about it, A.J.," Lynne said, giving him a scolding look.

"How about we show them this?" Sienna said, proudly displaying the ring to her mother.

Her mother squealed and all heads turned.

A.J. chuckled as he put his arm around Sienna and they went forward together.

* * * * *

*Don't miss the next woman
in the* WOMEN WHO DARE *miniseries…*
YOURS TO SEDUCE,
*Lana and Sean's story
is coming November 2003!*

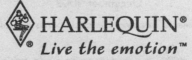

HARLEQUIN® Blaze™

In L.A., nothing remains confidential for long...

KISS & TELL

Don't miss

Tori Carrington's

exciting new miniseries featuring four
twentysomething friends—
and the secrets they *don't* keep.

Look for:

#105—NIGHT FEVER
October 2003

#109—FLAVOR OF THE MONTH
November 2003

#113—JUST BETWEEN US...
December 2003

Available wherever Harlequin books are sold.

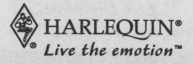

HARLEQUIN®
Live the emotion™

HARLEQUIN® *Blaze*™

In September 2003

Look for the latest sizzling sensation from
USA TODAY bestselling author

Suzanne Forster

BRIEF ENCOUNTERS

When Swan McKenna's accused of stealing five million dollars
from her racy men's underwear company, Brief Encounters,
a federal agent moves in on the place and on her. With his
government-issue good looks, little does Swan expect by-
the-book Rob Gaines to help her out by reluctantly agreeing
to strut his stuff in her upcoming fashion show. Nor does
she realize that once she sees Rob in his underwear, she
won't be able to resist catching him out of it....

And that their encounters will be anything but brief!

*Don't miss this superspecial Blaze™ volume #101
at your favorite local retailer.*

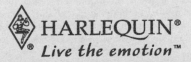

HARLEQUIN®
Live the emotion™

COMING NEXT MONTH

#105 NIGHT FEVER Tori Carrington
Kiss & Tell, Bk.1
Four friends. Countless secrets... Dr. Layla Hollister doesn't think she
has any secrets worth telling...until she throws caution to the winds and
indulges in an incredible one-night stand with a sexy stranger. A no-strings
encounter—exactly what the doctor ordered. That is, until Layla walks into
the clinic the next morning and discovers her mystery lover is really
her new boss. And he's expecting to pick up where they left off....

#106 PACKED WITH PLEASURE Lori Wilde
Gorgeous, confident Alec Ramsey—to fire up *her* engines?
Eden Montgomery's sure hoping so. He's exactly the adventure-hungry
daredevil she needs. Having lost her creative edge, she's counting on a
superhot tryst with Alec to not only inspire her sexy, one-of-a-kind gift
baskets, but her sexy, one-of-a-kind self!

#107 WICKED GAMES Alison Kent
www.girl-gear, Bk.2
gIRL-gEAR VP Kinsey Gray is not pleased to hear that Doug Storey
is moving away to Denver. She and the sexy architect have a history,
but Kinsey was never quite sure how she felt about him. Now that he's
leaving, it's time she made up her mind. With the help of a three-step plan
to seduce Doug, Kinsey's positive she'll persuade him to stick around. The
wicked games she has planned for him will knock *more* than his socks off!

#108 GIRL'S GUIDE TO HUNTING & KISSING Joanne Rock
Single in South Beach, Bk. 2
When Summer Farnsworth goes hunting for the perfect man to have a little
fling with, Jackson Taggart is not who she had in mind. There's not a rebel
bone—or a tattoo—under those too-starched shirts, or so she thinks. But
whoever said opposites attract must know something. Because after a few
long, steamy kisses, Summer has discovered a *big* attraction to the button-
down type.

Visit us at www.eHarlequin.com